PERIL AT GRANITE PEAK

HARDY BOYS ADVENTURES™

#5 *PERIL AT GRANITE PEAK*

FRANKLIN W. DIXON

ALADDIN   New York London Toronto Sydney New Delhi

ALADDIN
An imprint of Simon & Schuster Children's Publishing Division
1230 Avenue of the Americas, New York, NY 10020
First Aladdin hardcover edition February 2014
Text copyright © 2014 by Simon & Schuster, Inc.
Jacket illustration copyright © 2014 by Kevin Keele
Jacket design by Karin Paprocki
For information about special discounts for bulk purchases, please contact Simon & Schuster Special Sales at 1-866-506-1949 or business@simonandschuster.com.
The Simon & Schuster Speakers Bureau can bring authors to your live event.
For more information or to book an event contact the Simon & Schuster Speakers Bureau at 1-866-248-3049 or visit our website at www.simonspeakers.com.
The text of this book was set in Adobe Caslon Pro.
Manufactured in the United States of America 0114 FFG
2 4 6 8 10 9 7 5 3 1
Library of Congress Control Number 2013026397
ISBN 978-1-4424-9396-4 (hc)
ISBN 978-1-4424-9395-7 (pbk)
ISBN 978-1-4424-9397-1 (eBook)

CONTENTS

PERIL AT GRANITE PEAK

GOING DOWNHILL

1

FRANK

HEADS UP, FRANK!" JOE SHOUTED. "Coming through!"

I glanced up from adjusting my boot buckle. My ski helmet made it hard to see. But my brother was impossible to miss in his red-and-blue jacket and tricked-out mirrored goggles. He bent low over his skis, poles tucked tightly under his arms and a big grin on his face.

"Learn to steer or you'll be back on the bunny slope, hotshot!" I yelled with a laugh as he whizzed past me.

Then I looked over my shoulder to check on our friend Chet Morton. Chet was the reason Joe and I were in Vermont, but that didn't mean he was an expert skier. Not even close. My eyes widened as Chet's skis almost crossed while he was negotiating an easy turn. He lurched and started to fall, but somehow righted himself.

"Nice save, buddy!" I called helpfully.

Chet turned his head and squinted at me. It looked like his goggles were crooked. He was picking up speed as he slid downhill.

Just ahead, Joe had executed a crisp stop and was looking back as well. "Look out, Chet!" he hollered. "Tree!"

Chet whipped his head around just in time to see the huge spruce hurtling at him. Well, technically he was hurtling at it. Whatever. The effect would be the same if the two collided.

"Turn! Turn!" Joe and I yelled at the same time.

Chet leaned hard to the left, missing the tree by inches. Whew! He lost his balance immediately after that, belly flopping into a large snowdrift.

"Close one," Joe called.

"Yeah." I frowned, tilting my head as I heard a weird rumble. "What was that?"

Then I saw my answer. The snowdrift Chet had hit was moving.

"Avalanche!" Joe shouted. "Get out of the way, bro!"

He pushed off, aiming straight down the slope. I did the same. Glancing back over my shoulder, I saw Chet scrambling to his feet on the uphill side of the moving mass of tumbling snow. Good. He was safe. Joe and me? Not so much.

There was a snow-covered pile of rocks just ahead so I bent low, leaning into a tidy parallel turn to avoid it. I looked over, expecting Joe to follow. But he was still heading straight down.

"Look out!" I yelled.

Too late. Joe was headed straight for the rocks! And the avalanche was coming fast. If he wiped out, he'd be buried!

I held my breath as Joe reached the rock pile. He saw it a half second before he got there and bent a little lower, letting gravity take him up and over on its thin covering of snow. A second later he was airborne. One ski started to dip down, and for a second I was sure he was going to wipe out. But he recovered quickly, landing hard but squarely and then turning sharply to follow me out of the path of the avalanche.

Joe was breathing hard when he caught up to me at the base of the slope. "Nice skiing, brother," he said, lifting his fist.

I bumped it, then pushed back my goggles. "Nice jump," I said. "That was a little too close for comfort."

"Where's Chet?" Joe peered up the slope. The avalanche was over, and we saw Chet carefully snowplowing his way down the hill.

By the time he reached us, my hands had almost stopped shaking. "Are you guys okay?" Chet cried. "I didn't mean to do that!"

"Forget it," I told him. "We're fine. It's just lucky nobody else was on the trail when it happened."

Chet nodded. "Yeah. This place is even deader than Cody said it would be."

There were maybe three or four skiers visible on the various hills within our view, plus half a dozen beginners on the bunny slope over near the lodge. Other than that, we had the mountain to ourselves.

Joe was already heading for the lift. "Let's try the White Rattlesnake Trail next. Cody was telling us about it at breakfast, remember? It sounds like fun."

I didn't answer for a second. The White Rattlesnake did sound like fun. Maybe a little too much fun for Chet. If he'd caused an avalanche on the relatively easy green circle trail we'd just negotiated, what would he do on a trickier slope?

But Chet wasn't saying anything, so I didn't either. Joe and I might be brothers, but that didn't mean we always saw things the same way. He was definitely the daredevil type. Me? I liked a little adrenaline rush as much as the next guy—as long as that next guy wasn't Joe. He already thought I was way too cautious. I didn't want to give him more ammunition. Besides, Chet was a big boy. If he didn't want to try the White Rattlesnake Trail, he could speak up and say so.

We were a dozen yards from the lift when we heard a bark. Glancing over, I saw a guy hurrying past, head down and hands shoved into the pockets of his well-worn parka. A large black-and-tan dog was at his side. Her ears were pricked toward us, and her furry tail was wagging.

"Cody!" Chet called, waving. "Yo, over here!"

Cody Gallagher was the one who'd invited us to Granite Peak Lodge. He'd been Chet's camp counselor years ago, and the two of them had kept in touch. Cody was a few years older than us, tall and wiry with reddish-brown hair. A little quiet, but a nice guy. He'd graduated from high school a year or two earlier and now worked full-time at the lodge with his parents. His trusty Lab-shepherd mix, Blizzard, never left his side.

Cody heard Chet and looked over. He was pretty far away, but for a split second it looked as if a shadow passed over his expression. Was I imagining things, or did he appear less than thrilled to see us?

But the moment passed quickly. "Hi, guys," Cody said, coming over. "Having fun?"

"A blast," Joe replied, leaning over to rub Blizzard's furry head.

I nodded. "But listen, there was a minor avalanche on the Sugar Maple Trail just now. . . ." I quickly filled him in on what had happened.

Cody listened, looking concerned. "I'll let my parents know," he said. "They might want to add that slope to the restricted list until we can check it out."

I nodded again. There was a notice hanging on the bulletin board in the lodge's dining room, listing several ski trails that were off-limits due to weather conditions or other issues. I'd had plenty of time to study it that morning while

5

Joe and Chet were having a third helping of bacon and eggs.

"So where are you going?" Chet asked Cody as we neared the ski lift. "Hoping to get a few runs in?"

"Not exactly," Cody said. "Mom asked me to clear some branches off one of the trails."

There were only a few people waiting for the lifts. As we arrived, a young couple hopped into an empty car. Cody grabbed a well-worn pair of skis and poles that were leaning against the wall of the control booth.

"Guess we won't have to wait long for a lift," Joe joked as two more skiers stepped into another lift.

Cody grimaced. "Yeah."

I shot Joe a warning look. Leave it to my brother to bring up a sore subject. We all knew that Granite Peak Lodge was having trouble attracting enough visitors—that was the main reason we were there. A couple of bigger, flashier resorts had opened on the other side of the mountain recently, and people were flocking to them. According to Cody's dad, the skiing was better on this side of the mountain, but people liked the Wi-Fi and spa treatments and fancy gourmet food those other resorts offered.

That was why Cody had e-mailed Chet a few weeks ago, urging him to come for a stay over winter break and bring all his friends. He'd even sent a discount coupon for one of the lodge's nicest suites.

Chet had been all for it. Surprisingly, so had his parents. Or maybe not so surprisingly. They were going to a wedding out of state, and I guess they preferred to ship Chet out to the lodge rather than leave him home alone.

However, Joe and I were the only friends Chet could convince to tag along. I guess nobody else's parents liked the idea of a bunch of teen guys let loose at a ski resort.

That hadn't been a problem for us, though. Mom and Dad had okayed the plan as soon as they heard about it. And I was pretty sure I knew why. See, Joe and I had this hobby—solving crimes. We'd been doing it since we were little kids. And we were good at it. We'd nabbed more than our share of bad guys, sometimes with the help of our dad, a retired police detective and private investigator. Dad didn't always approve of our tendency to put ourselves in danger, but he'd been mostly supportive of our sleuthing. He got it, you know?

But lately we'd run into some trouble. Legal trouble, mostly. Not to mention some bad feelings with the local police. Long story short, we'd had to promise to get out of the crime-solving business for good, or we'd end up in reform school.

After we'd helped bust a local crime ring called the Red Arrow, though, Bayport's police chief (and our parents) relaxed the rules, telling us we could catch a few crooks now and then as long as we agreed to keep law enforcement in the loop. Still, we were trying to keep a low profile in the crime-solving department. Truth be told, I think our parents were hoping that getting us out of Bayport for a week or two might keep our minds off mysteries for a while.

And I figured they were right. What kind of trouble could we find up here?

Soon we were at the front of the line. The lifts only held two people apiece.

"Go ahead," I told Chet as an empty car swung toward us. "Joe and I will catch the next one."

My brother and I watched as Chet and Cody headed up the mountain. A moment later we hopped onto the next lift, our skis swinging as the car rose into the crisp, cold winter air.

"This is awesome." Joe scanned the scenery. "I can't believe we've got this whole place to ourselves, pretty much."

"Yeah, you might want to stop mentioning that in front of Cody," I told him. "Especially after that weather forecast this morning."

Joe's face fell. "Oh yeah," he said. "Do you think we'll have to leave?"

I shrugged. The weather report was warning that a serious blizzard might be coming in the next forty-eight hours. For a while they'd thought it would skirt the area, but now it seemed to be aiming right at Granite Peak. Then again, there was still a slight chance it would all peter out. I supposed that was why my aunt Trudy called them "weather guessers."

"Not much we can do about the weather," I told Joe. "Let's just have fun and see what happens. We can make a decision tomorrow."

Chet and Cody were waiting when we arrived at the top. The lift dropped us off at the edge of a large, flat clearing near the top of the hill. Several trails started there, snaking off in different directions, with large wooden signs marking the start of each one. The signs included the trail's name, difficulty level, and a map showing its place on the mountain. A trio of twentysomething girls who'd been just ahead of us in the lift line were starting out down a black diamond trail, while a man dressed in a flashy red-and-white parka was standing nearby, adjusting his helmet and goggles.

"Great day for skiing, huh?" I said as I passed him.

The man turned and blinked at me through his goggles. He was in his early thirties, with pasty skin, thin brown hair poking out from under his helmet, and watery gray eyes. He turned away without bothering to respond.

Whatever. I shrugged and moved on.

"White Rattlesnake, here we come!" Joe exclaimed, using his poles to push himself along in the direction of the trailhead.

"Hang on, I think my buckle's loose." Chet knelt down and fiddled with one of his boots.

"Have fun, you guys," Cody said. "I'll catch you at dinner." He headed toward one of the trailheads with Blizzard at his heels.

While we waited for Chet, I watched the pasty-skinned man head across the clearing. He wasn't exactly an expert skier. He almost tripped over his poles, then got his skis crossed and almost went down. I was a little surprised he wasn't still taking lessons down on the bunny slope.

As he reached one of the signs, I glanced at it. Good. It was a green circle trail—the easiest level.

But my eyes widened when I took in the name on the sign: Whispering Pine Trail.

"Wait! No!" I yelled as the man pushed off and disappeared down the slope. I spun around and gestured to the others. "We have to stop him!"

RESCUE 2

JOE

THE WHITE RATTLESNAKE TRAIL LOOKED epic. I couldn't wait to tackle it. I was totally focused on it when Frank started yelling.

He was jumping around like his ski pants were on fire. Frank wasn't usually the excitable type, so I figured something was up.

"What's wrong?" I called, skiing over. Cody was about to set off down a different trail, but he turned to look at Frank too.

"That trail!" Frank cried, pointing to a sign marking one of the trailheads nearby. "A guy just went down it. But it's on the list—it's supposed to be closed!"

"Huh?" Chet stopped messing with his boots and stood up. "But there's no closed sign." He gestured at a different trail sign, which had a big, bright-orange ribbon with the words CLOSED TRAIL tied diagonally across it.

But Cody looked grim. "No, Frank's right," he said, skiing over to join us. "That trail should definitely be closed. Ice."

Now I got it. Frank was—hmm, how can I put this?—a little bit of a nerd. Okay, maybe more than a little bit. But the guy was smart, and he had a memory like that of an elephant. I'd noticed him studying the lodge's bulletin board at breakfast. No surprise that he'd memorized it.

"Ice is bad news," I said. "I'm on it!"

I pushed off, heading down the slope at top speed. Behind me, I heard the others doing the same. At least I assumed that was what was going on. I didn't bother to look back, since I'd just spotted the guy Frank had mentioned.

Yeah, definitely a beginner. He was wobbling and clutching his poles like lifelines, slowing himself down every few yards with awkward snowplow stops.

"Stop!" I yelled as I skied toward him. "Hey, you!"

The guy glanced back at me. Instead of stopping, he pushed off with both poles, picking up speed as he turned and headed straight down the hill. What was he doing?

"Seriously!" I shouted. "Hold up a sec, okay?"

This time he didn't even look back. Tucking my poles under my arms, I crouched down, picking up speed on the fairly gentle slope.

I whipped around a few easy turns, gaining on the guy all the time. As we reached another straightaway, I pulled even with him.

"Listen!" I called, raising my voice over the wind whistling past my ears. "You have to stop. There's ice ahead!"

He shot me a look. I couldn't read his expression behind his goggles.

"Who are you? Leave me alone!" he yelled.

I blew out a quick, frustrated sigh. Was this guy dense, or what?

"Stop!" I shouted. "Ice!"

I glanced ahead, wondering exactly where the ice might be. Oops. There it was—just a few dozen yards ahead. I could see where the snow must have melted and then frozen up again; there was a distinct sheen that caught the sun and made me squint even with goggles on. The ice patch didn't look very big—I doubted they'd even bother to close a more advanced trail for that sort of thing.

But this was a beginner trail. And the guy beside me barely even qualified as a beginner. His skis were already looking crooked—if he hit that ice at the speed he was going, he could break a leg. Or two. Or maybe his head.

"Stop!" I yelled once more, gesturing wildly with both poles. "Seriously, dude!"

No response. We were almost to the ice patch. Enough talking; time for action.

I tilted into a steep carve turn, aiming right at the other skier. At the same time, I dragged my poles to slow myself down a little.

"Oof!" the guy grunted as I plowed into him.

We both flew sideways and landed in the soft snow at the edge of the trail. I did my best to avoid the other guy, though I clipped his helmet with my elbow. That was going to leave a bruise.

The guy spit out a mouthful of snow. "Hey!" he cried. "What's your problem?"

"That!" I pointed at the ice, which was less than ten feet away. "Didn't you hear me telling you to stop? This trail's supposed to be closed!"

The man frowned. "I didn't see anything about that on the sign."

"Yeah, well, that's why I came after you." I glanced up as Cody and Frank slid to a stop beside us. A little farther up the hill, Chet was making his way down more slowly. Cody's dog, Blizz, was bounding through the snow at Chet's side.

"Is everyone okay?" Cody asked breathlessly.

"Think so." I stood and brushed off the snow. All my bones seemed to be in one piece. I offered a hand to help the guy up, but he ignored it.

"This is outrageous," he told Cody. "I thought this establishment advertised its good safety record! How can that be when you have hooligans crashing into your guests?"

Hooligans? Nice way to treat the guy who just saved your life. Or your femur. Whatever. But never mind—I'd been called worse.

Cody looked at me nervously. "Joe was just trying to help,

Mr. Wright," he said. "You could have been badly hurt on that ice."

Mr. Wright looked down at the ice. "Well, why wasn't the trail properly marked, then?" he blustered, climbing to his feet. "I could have been killed!"

I rolled my eyes at Frank behind Mr. Wright's back. Killed? Maybe an overstatement. Frank frowned at me.

"That's a good point," he said to Cody. "What happened to the sign?"

"I don't know." Cody shrugged. "I helped Dad mark the off-limits trails myself this morning."

Mr. Wright was glaring from me to Cody and back again. If looks could kill, we'd both be in trouble. Maybe it was time to get out of Dodge.

I grabbed my poles, which I'd dropped in the crash. "Let's go check out the sign situation," I told Frank. "Maybe we can figure out what happened."

Chet reached us in time to hear me. He shot me and Frank a dubious glance. "You mean—you guys want to go investigate?"

I rolled my eyes again. "Not investigate," I said. "Just check on things. See if we can tell where that closed sign went."

"Yeah." Chet smirked. "Like I said. Investigate."

Cody and Mr. Wright looked a little confused. Ignoring Chet, I glanced at my brother. "Come on, Frank. Feel like a hike?"

Frank and I kicked off our skis and started climbing back up the hill, leaving Cody and Chet to deal with Mr. Wright. "Nice guy," Frank muttered as soon as we were out of earshot.

I grinned. "Yeah. So what do you think happened to the sign?"

He shrugged. "Probably just an oversight. Cody and his folks seem pretty stressed out right now, what with this possible blizzard chasing away their guests. Maybe they forgot one of the signs, or didn't tie it on tightly enough."

"Maybe." We didn't talk much after that. As it turns out, hiking up a mountain through knee-deep snow is a lot harder than skiing down it.

By the time we reached the top, we were both panting. There was no sign of that orange ribbon on or near the sign.

"Guess you were right," I told Frank, already losing interest. "Probably never got marked in the first place." I glanced toward the White Rattlesnake Trail. Maybe we could get in a run before Chet caught up. That might be for the best— Chet was definitely a better skier than Mr. Wright, but he might not be a match for anything beyond a green circle hill.

"Hold on." Something in Frank's voice made me turn right away.

"What?"

"Check this out." He waved me over.

I saw what he was looking at immediately. The top of the Whispering Pine Trail sign had about a half-inch layer of snow on it—the result of some midmorning flurries. But there was one spot that was clean.

"That's just about where the 'Closed' ribbon would have gone," I said.

"Right. So what happened to it?" Frank was already looking around.

I did the same, stepping over to peer into a snow-covered tangle of bushes near the sign. Spotting a flash of color, I pushed the branches aside.

"Aha! Here it is. Think it blew off?" I reached for the orange ribbon. When I tugged on it, it didn't budge.

Frank looked over my shoulder. "Looks like it's being held down by a rock." He glanced at me, looking grim. "You know what this means, right?"

"It didn't blow off," I said slowly. "Someone took it down on purpose!"

WEATHER WARNING

3

FRANK

JOE KICKED THE ROCK OFF THE WARN-
ing ribbon. "Should we put it back up?" he asked.

"Definitely." I grabbed the ribbon and wrapped it around the sign, making sure it was secure.

Joe watched me. "So who do you think dumped that in the bushes? And why?"

"I don't know." I brushed off my gloves.

"Let's go tell Cody's parents what happened."

Fifteen minutes later we were in the lodge's main office. Cody's father was there, sorting through some paperwork. He was a tall, broad-shouldered man with weather-beaten skin, a bristly salt-and-pepper beard, and a quick smile. But that smile faded when he heard about Mr. Wright's near miss on the slopes.

"If something like this had to happen, why did it have to happen to Stanley Wright?" he commented with a grimace. "That man hasn't been happy with a single thing since he arrived." Mr. Gallagher sighed and shot us a look. "Sorry. Not very professional of me to say that."

"No, we get it," Joe said. "The dude practically accused me of assaulting him when all I was doing was trying to keep him from breaking his neck."

"So about the closed sign . . . ," I began.

"It's probably nothing," Mr. Gallagher said. "An animal might have knocked it loose. Or maybe the wind."

"I don't think so, sir," I said. "The snow was only disturbed in that one spot. It looked like someone just lifted the ribbon right off."

"Hmm." Mr. Gallagher rubbed his beard. "Well, in that case it was probably a prank. We have several rather, er, lively younger kids staying here right now. I'll look into it. Thanks for letting me know, boys."

"You're welcome," Joe said.

I nodded, feeling uneasy. Mr. Gallagher didn't seem to be taking this incident very seriously. What if someone was trying to sabotage his business? Maybe someone from one of those rival resorts across the mountain?

Then I realized I probably shouldn't be worrying about this kind of thing anymore.

"Okay," I said. "I guess we'll get back out there, then. Coming, Joe?"

• • •

Joe, Chet, and I spent the next several hours out on the slopes. After a few runs down White Rattlesnake and a couple of other trails, Joe talked us into taking a snowboarding lesson. Our teacher was Cody's mom, a petite, energetic woman who soon had us practicing our heel and toe side turns, our glides, and our stops. When she was convinced we wouldn't kill ourselves, she took us out on the real slopes to practice. It was fun, but exhausting.

So by the time we hit the dining room that evening, we were all ravenous. "I hope the food comes fast," Chet said, tucking his napkin into his collar like a little kid. "I'm so hungry I could eat this plate!"

Our waitress arrived just in time to hear him. She was probably only a couple of years older than us, with curly brown hair and a pretty face. Her name tag identified her as Josie Lambert.

"Please don't eat the plates, guys," she said with a laugh, setting a basket of freshly baked rolls on our table. "I'll do my best to get your dinner here fast."

Joe grabbed a roll and grinned at her. "Cool. Because the bread basket's only going to last about thirty seconds with Chet around."

"Hey!" Chet mumbled through the roll he'd just stuffed in his mouth. "I can't help it. I'm a growing boy."

Josie giggled. "I'll make sure to let the chef know she shouldn't skimp on your portion."

"Mine either," I said, patting my stomach.

"Yeah. In fact, you can tell her to make it a double all around." Joe glanced around the dining room. "There should be plenty of extra food back there. This place is even emptier than it was last night."

Josie's smile suddenly collapsed. "I know, right?" she moaned. "Everyone is totally panicking about the weather. Before long there won't be any guests left! And the Gallaghers definitely don't need that right now."

How does Josie know about the trouble the Gallaghers are having getting guests? I wondered. But before I could ask her about it, there was an angry shout from across the room.

"What's going on over there?" Chet wondered as he reached for a second roll.

I was already leaning sideways in my chair to see past Joe. Two men were getting in each other's faces over near the entrance.

"Whoa," Chet said. "Isn't that what's-his-name from earlier? Joe's crash test dummy?"

"Stanley Wright," I said. "Who's the other guy?"

I glanced at Josie, but she wasn't paying any attention to us anymore. She was staring at the two men, looking worried.

"Oh no," she muttered. Without another word, she ran off toward the kitchen.

Joe shrugged. "I don't know who the other guy is. But he looks like he could squash our pal Stanley like a bug."

He had a point. The second man was a tall, buff-looking guy in his late twenties. Based on his build, he was no stranger to the gym. He had to have a good fifty or sixty pounds on Stanley Wright. All of it muscle.

"Should we go over there and try to break it up?" Joe said.

Before Chet or I could answer, a man burst out of the kitchen. I vaguely recognized him as a lodge employee—he'd helped carry our bags in from Chet's car when we'd arrived the day before. He was in his forties, almost as tall as Mr. Muscles but a lot leaner. Still, he looked like the kind of guy you didn't want to mess with, if you know what I mean.

"That's enough, guys." The employee's gruff voice wasn't very loud, but it carried. "Break it up."

The taller man immediately took a step back. "Sorry," he told the employee. "Just a little difference of opinion, that's all." He glared at Stanley Wright. "Just stay out of my face, dude," he snapped. "Or else!" He turned on his heel and stomped out of the dining room.

"Wow, that Stanley makes friends everywhere he goes, doesn't he?" Joe said.

"Yeah." I'd just spotted Cody's mom hurrying toward our table, followed by a young woman in her twenties with sleek dark hair pulled back in a ponytail.

"Hello, boys," Mrs. Gallagher greeted us. "Having an early dinner, huh?"

Chet patted his belly. "Yeah. Snowboarding really works up an appetite."

"We had a blast today, though," I said. "We can't wait to get out there again tomorrow."

"Yeah." Joe grinned. "I can't speak for these two, but I'm thinking I'll be ready to enter the next Winter Olympics any day now."

Mrs. Gallagher chuckled, but she looked distracted. She shot a slightly worried look at the TV hanging over the bar at one end of the room. It was tuned to the weather forecast.

"Yes, well, I hope the storm holds off so you can keep enjoying the slopes," she said. "In the meantime, I'd like you boys to meet another guest—this is Miss Poppy Song. She's on her own tonight, and I thought maybe you wouldn't mind if she joined you."

"Sure thing." I gestured to the empty chair between me and Joe. "Have a seat."

"Thanks." Poppy smiled gratefully at Mrs. Gallagher, then turned her bright, intelligent brown eyes to us as the lodge owner hurried off. "I'd feel like a total nerd sitting by myself."

"Then why'd you come skiing by yourself?" Chet helped himself to another roll, then pushed the almost-empty basket toward her.

"I didn't. I was here with a group of friends, but they all chickened out when they heard about this blizzard that's supposed to hit tomorrow night." Poppy selected a roll. "They left a couple of hours ago."

"And you stayed?" Joe asked.

Poppy shrugged. "I didn't have much choice. My apartment's being fumigated, so I can't go home. I figured I'd rather ride out the storm here than get stuck sleeping on someone's couch."

"So this blizzard is really coming, huh?" I glanced again at the TV, but we were too far away to hear what the reporter was saying.

Our waitress, Josie, arrived back at the table just in time to hear me. "We don't know that yet," she said quickly, passing out glasses of water to all four of us. "It's still possible it could miss us. Anyway, they're expecting an update to the forecast in a little while. Until then, you should just relax and not worry about it, okay?"

"Sure, whatever," Chet said. "I'm ready to order if you guys are."

We placed our dinner orders, and Josie hurried away. Poppy took a sip of her water and glanced around the table.

"So now you know my story," she said cheerfully. "What about you guys? Where are you from? How'd you end up here at Granite Peak Lodge?"

"Cody Gallagher—he's the owners' son, you know—was my camp counselor back in the day," Chet said. "He invited me up here."

"Old friends with the owners' son, huh? Interesting." Poppy glanced at Joe and me. "What about you two? Did you go to camp with Cody Gallagher too?"

"Nope. We go to high school with Chet," I said.

Joe grinned. "Yeah. And we're the only ones he could sucker into making the long drive up here in his old jalopy."

"Very funny." Chet frowned while Joe and I laughed. He was almost ridiculously proud of the junked-out old yellow roadster he'd fixed up himself. "The Queen doesn't appreciate your insults."

"The Queen?" Poppy laughed. "Do you mean your car? Why do you call it that?"

"Because he's nuts," Joe informed her.

Just then someone on the far side of the room let out a sharp whistle. Glancing over, I saw Mr. Gallagher standing near the bar, staring up at the TV.

"Hey, could everyone pipe down for a second?" he called out as the room went quiet. "They're about to update the forecast."

Someone turned up the volume on the TV. The reporter's voice boomed out at us, sounding solemn and excited at the same time. Apparently the weather guessers had made up their minds: the blizzard was definitely headed our way.

And it was shaping up to be the Storm of the Century!

EXIT PLAN 4

JOE

SURE WE DON'T HAVE TIME FOR ONE more run?" I glanced over at the ski lift. There had been a few other people on the slopes that morning, but with each passing hour the numbers dwindled. Now car after car went clanking up the hill empty, and there was nobody waiting in line.

Frank checked his watch. "Better not. We've got a long drive ahead of us, and we don't want to take a chance of getting caught out on the roads when things get bad."

That was my brother—Mr. Cautious. Mr. Responsible. Mr. Annoying. But in this case, I knew he was probably right. With the blizzard due to hit in a few hours, it was time to go.

Chet stuck out his tongue, catching a few flakes. It had started snowing lightly about an hour ago. According to the weather report we'd watched at lunchtime, the snow would start picking up within the next couple of hours and hit blizzard conditions soon after dark. And by the end, it could bring a whopping thirty inches of the stuff!

Yeah, it was definitely time to go.

We dropped off our skis and other rented gear at the equipment shed. Mr. Gallagher was there overseeing things.

"Taking off, boys?" he asked as he stacked Chet's skis against the wall.

"Uh-huh. We figured we'd better hit the road before the storm gets bad," Frank said.

The lodge owner smiled, though it looked a little forced. "Can't say I blame you. This storm looks to be a monster. Hope you'll come back another time, though."

"We will," I promised. "This place is great."

We headed into the main building. A roaring fire cast its glow over the spacious lobby. A bunch of people were over there, warming their hands and chattering excitedly about the coming storm. Several small children chased one another around the pile of luggage near the door, shrieking at the tops of their lungs.

"Looks like most people are on their way out," Chet said. "We should hurry."

Our suite was at the far end of the hallway upstairs. As

we reached it, the door opened and Josie hurried out with an armful of crumpled towels.

"Oh!" she exclaimed, stopping just in time to avoid running into us. "Sorry, didn't see you coming."

"What, did Chet order room service when we weren't looking?" I joked.

Josie blinked, looking confused. "Huh?"

"You're a waitress," I said. "Waitresses bring food, right?"

"Oh!" Her expression cleared, and she laughed. "Yes, I'm a waitress during mealtimes. The rest of the time I'm a maid. I was just making up your rooms for the night." She shrugged. "The lodge is on a pretty tight budget these days, so we're all pulling double duty."

"Wow." I was a little surprised. "Okay, so Cody mentioned business has dropped off lately. But this place must still bring in the big bucks, right?"

Josie hesitated, looking uncertain. "Um, not exactly," she said at last. "I mean, I probably shouldn't talk about this with guests, but since you guys are friends with Cody . . ."

"What is it?" Chet looked concerned. "Is the lodge really in that much trouble?"

Josie glanced up and down the hallway. "Sort of," she said, lowering her voice. "Ever since those other resorts opened across the mountain, things have been pretty tight around here." She bit her lip, which was quivering slightly. "If it gets any worse, I'm afraid I might not have a job much longer!"

I hated seeing a pretty girl look so upset. But I wasn't sure what to say to cheer her up.

"It'll be all right," Frank said. "Business has to pick up again soon, right?"

Josie shrugged. "I hope so. But this blizzard isn't helping, you know? Everyone's leaving!" She sighed, blowing a strand of curly hair off her face. "At least you guys are still here, though."

Frank, Chet, and I traded a guilty look. "Um, not exactly," Frank said. "We were just coming upstairs to pack."

"Really?" Josie's face fell. "Are you sure? I mean, the storm might not be as bad as they're saying. You know how those weather people like to exaggerate. We'll probably only get a few inches!"

"Maybe," Frank said. "That's not what the weather forecast is saying, though."

"They don't know everything!" Josie was starting to look and sound kind of crazed. "Seriously, this is a ski lodge. Snow is a good thing, right?"

"Sure." Chet backed up a step. "Um, but my car doesn't have snow tires, and—"

"Everything okay over here?" a gruff voice interrupted.

I spun around, startled. The employee who'd broken up that fight last night was standing right behind us. Talk about stealthy! I hadn't even heard him coming.

"It's nothing, Rick," Josie said quickly, squeezing the towels more tightly in her arms. "We were just talking."

I glanced at the man's name tag. It read Rick Ferguson.

He caught my eye. "I hear you boys are taking off soon," he said.

"Yeah." I wondered if he was going to start begging us to stay too.

Instead he nodded curtly. "Let me know if you need any help getting your bags downstairs." Then he glanced at Josie. "Mrs. G was looking for you down in the kitchen."

"Okay." Josie scurried off. Rick nodded at us again, then followed her more slowly.

"Wow," Chet said as we pushed through the door to our suite, which was standing ajar. "Josie seemed really bummed out about this whole blizzard thing."

Frank stepped over to the closet and pulled out his suitcase. "Can you blame her? It sounds like things are pretty bad for the lodge right now."

"Maybe that's how that warning ribbon went missing yesterday," Chet said. He grabbed a crumpled pair of jeans off the floor where he'd dropped them the night before. "Too few people trying to do too many things."

"Maybe." I traded a look with Frank, realizing we'd never filled Chet in on what we'd found in the bushes. Just as well. He'd probably accuse us of looking for a mystery where there wasn't one.

Or was there? Even if the warning ribbon could have blown off into the bushes, that rock definitely hadn't rolled itself on top of it.

"Yeah, maybe." Frank shot a look at the window. The

curtains were pulled back, allowing us to see the fat, lazy snowflakes drifting steadily to earth. "But come on, let's get going before the storm gets any worse."

I pushed all thoughts of missing ribbons out of my mind. It didn't matter now. We were leaving.

Fifteen minutes later we were back in the lobby. Chet dropped a duffel bag atop our pile of luggage, then fished his car keys out of his pocket.

"Let's find Cody and say good-bye," he said. "Then I'll bring the car around and we can load our stuff."

"Sounds like a plan." I glanced around and spotted Cody right away. He was perched on an overstuffed leather armchair near the fireplace, watching those rowdy little kids we'd seen earlier. There were three boys and a girl, ranging in age from five-ish on down to barely walking. All four of them were clustered around Blizzard, patting her on the head or tugging on her shaggy fur. Her brown eyes had a soft, patient look as she nosed at one of the boys.

Cody spotted us coming and stood up. "You guys taking off?" he asked.

"Yeah. Sorry," Chet said.

Cody shrugged. "No, it's okay. Seriously." He smiled. "Trust me, I wouldn't expect you to stay through the Blizzard of the Century or whatever they're calling it." He glanced around the lobby. "I'm surprised a few people are actually planning to ride it out here. Even most of the staff has already cut out."

He sounded resigned to the situation. "Yeah. Well, thanks for inviting us," Frank said. "It was good meeting you."

"Right," I put in. "Don't worry, we'll be back."

"Cool." Cody smiled and lifted a hand to high-five all three of us. "Safe driving, okay?"

I laughed. "Easier said than done with Chet behind the wheel."

Cody chuckled. "Some things never change." He elbowed Chet. "Remember that time at camp when you crashed your bike into the—"

"Kids? There you are!" He was interrupted by a harried-looking woman in her midthirties. She hurried over and grabbed a couple of the kids. "Leave the poor dog alone and find your shoes. Daddy's almost packed up."

"Do you need any help, Mrs. Richmond?" Cody asked politely.

We drifted away toward the entrance. "So what'd you crash into at camp?" I asked Chet.

"The head counselor." Chet's cheeks went pink as Frank and I laughed. "But that was a long time ago. I'd better go fetch the Queen."

He disappeared through the big glass double doors leading outside. Frank and I wandered over to our little pile of luggage.

"Should we start dragging this stuff outside?" Frank suggested.

"Sure, why not."

Before long we'd transferred the entire pile to the sheltered pickup area right outside the main doors. I leaned against a column and watched a couple of cute college-aged girls with perky ponytails trying to shove a too-big duffel bag into the trunk of a subcompact.

Did I mention that Frank is kind of a nerd? He didn't even seem to notice the cute girls. Instead he was scanning the parking lot on the other side of the drive. There were only a few cars still parked over there. The snow was already starting to accumulate on top of them.

"What's taking Chet so long?" he wondered. "I can see his car from here."

I followed Frank's gaze. The yellow jalopy was sitting where we'd left it yesterday. I could see Chet inside, but so far the car wasn't moving.

"He's probably chatting with the Queen," I said. Then I stepped toward the college girls, who were still struggling with their bag. They really were awfully cute. And I wasn't one to ignore women in need. "Need some help with that, ladies?"

Just then Rick Ferguson appeared out of nowhere. "I've got it," he said in his gravelly voice. "Thanks."

"Sure." I watched as the employee managed to wedge the girls' bag into their trunk. As the girls climbed in and took off, I shifted my gaze to the fluffy flakes falling beyond the portico. "Snow's picking up," I commented.

"Yeah." Frank squinted at the parking lot. "Let's go hurry Chet along."

We headed out into the snow. I blinked as flakes blew into my face and stuck to my eyelashes. The temperature had dropped since we'd left the slopes, and the wind was picking up. I shoved my hands into my pockets as I walked.

When we reached the car, Chet rolled down the window. "What's the holdup?" I asked.

He looked sheepish. "The car won't start."

"What?" Frank frowned. "It was running fine two days ago!"

I smirked. "What do you expect from that old jalopy? I told you guys we should've borrowed Mom's car."

"It's probably nothing." Chet climbed out of the driver's seat. "Maybe a loose wire or something. Let me take a look."

He hurried around and opened the hood. "Come on, Joe," Frank said. "No sense all of us standing out here getting covered with snow."

"Come pick us up when you get her running again," I told Chet.

Cody and his father were just coming outside when Frank and I reached the portico. They both had several bags slung over their shoulders. An anxious-looking older couple emerged right behind them.

"Do you think it's too late?" the wife fretted. "I hope the roads aren't too bad yet."

"I'm sure it'll be fine, dear." Her husband cast a worried look at the cloud cover. "We have four-wheel drive. I'll go get the SUV."

Another group of departing guests burst out of the lodge, bringing a whoosh of warm air with them. Rick was with them, wheeling a hotel cart with several bags on it.

"I hope we're not in the way," Frank commented, kicking one of our duffels back a few feet.

"We wouldn't be if Chet could get that heap of spare parts moving already." I stepped forward, squinting through the steadily increasing snowfall. All I could see was a blob of yellow where the jalopy was. Still not moving.

As I turned back toward the lodge, I noticed a flash of movement in a first-floor window off to the left. It was Josie, the waitress-slash-maid. She was staring out at all the activity. It was hard to see clearly through the snow, but she looked kind of anxious. No wonder. The way she'd acted earlier, it had to be killing her to see so many people leaving at once.

"What were you looking at?" Frank asked when I rejoined him under the shelter of the portico.

I told him. "Maybe that's what happened to the Queen," I joked. "Josie seemed pretty freaked out about everyone leaving. Maybe she's sabotaging cars to keep people here."

"If so, the only one she got is Chet's." Frank watched as another car pulled away. "Anyway, the jalopy usually doesn't need any help to break down."

I grinned. "Good point." Squinting out into the snow, I spotted Chet walking toward us. "Uh-oh. This doesn't look like good news."

It wasn't. Chet had a hangdog look on his face that required no explanation.

"Sorry," he said, brushing snow off his hair. "It still won't start, and I can't figure out what's wrong."

Frank and I looked at each other. "Oh well," Frank said grimly. "Looks like we're going to have front-row seats to the Storm of the Century."

PLAN B 5

FRANK

JOE DIDN'T SEEM THAT UPSET ABOUT being stranded. He started chatting about whether the Gallaghers would let us try snowboarding during the blizzard. Yeah, right. If I had anything to say about it, that wouldn't be an option.

"Look, there's only one road off this mountain," I said. "That means everyone's going the same way. Maybe we can catch a ride at least as far as the nearest town with a car-rental place."

"Do you think so?" Chet looked hopeful.

"Can't hurt to ask." I hurried inside and looked around the lobby. It had cleared out a lot since the last time we were inside. Cody was over by the reception desk fiddling with the computer, and his dad was just disappearing up the stairs.

The only other people in sight were a young couple sitting on the wide stone hearth of the fireplace, sipping something out of chunky ceramic mugs. The male half of the couple was the guy we'd seen arguing with Stanley Wright the evening before.

I almost skipped talking to him. The guy seemed to have a serious temper. But this was no time to be choosy. I hurried over and introduced myself. Now I could tell what they were drinking—hot cocoa. The sweet scent tickled my nose and made me hungry.

"Nice to meet you, Frank." The man set down his mug, then stood and shook my hand. His grip was firm and his smile was friendly. "I'm Nate Katz, and this is my beautiful new bride, Cassie. We're here on our honeymoon."

Cassie smiled at me and said hello. She was gorgeous, with black hair and amber eyes.

"So what do you think about this blizzard, eh, Frank?" Nate asked, settling back into his seat. He seemed much more relaxed now than he had in the dining room last night. "Pretty exciting stuff."

"I guess." I looked at the snow falling outside. "Um, actually that's why I came over. Are you two planning to head out of here soon? Because our car broke down, and my friends and I are looking to hitch a ride down the mountain."

"Sorry, we'd be happy to help if we could." Nate took a sip of his cocoa. "But Cassie and I are staying put."

"Really? You're staying through the storm?" I was a

little surprised. Based on Josie's hysterical reaction earlier, I'd thought pretty much everyone was cutting out. Then again, Cody had said something about a few people sticking around.

"Yep, we're staying," Nate said. "Why not? This place runs on a generator—it's the only way to have power this far up the mountain."

"That also means the lodge shouldn't lose power even in a bad storm," Cassie spoke up.

"Right." Nate smiled at his bride. "Mr. Gallagher tells us he's got plenty of food laid in, and there'll be a skeleton staff staying here to keep things running smoothly. So anyone who wants to ride out the storm is welcome to stay."

Cassie nodded. "We don't want to cut our honeymoon short." She leaned closer to Nate. "It'll be extra romantic to be snowed in together."

"Definitely romantic." Nate set down his cocoa and put both arms around her, nuzzling her cheek.

Okay, the public display of affection was getting to be a little much for me. "Thanks anyway," I said. "Enjoy the rest of your honeymoon."

"We definitely will." Nate glanced up briefly. "Good luck finding a ride."

"Thanks." I stepped away. The sound of voices was coming from the hallway leading off toward the dining room, so I headed that way.

It was Stanley Wright. He was talking to Cody's mom.

Well, more like talking at her. It sounded like he was complaining about his room.

". . . and I also found a very mysterious stain on one of the pillowcases," he was saying. "What if I catch a disease or something? I have very sensitive skin, you know. I'm sure I mentioned that when I checked in."

"I'll speak to Josie about getting you a fresh set of pillowcases right away, Mr. Wright," Mrs. Gallagher said soothingly.

"Fine." Stanley frowned. "Now, about my towels—"

"Excuse me," I broke in. "Um, sorry to interrupt, but I have a question."

"Of course." Mrs. Gallagher looked relieved. "What is it, Frank?"

"Actually, my question is for Mr. Wright." I forced a smile as I glanced at the man. It wouldn't be pleasant sharing a car with him all the way down the mountain, but like I said, things were kind of desperate. "I was just wondering if you were planning to leave soon, because I—"

I didn't get to finish the question. "No, I'm not planning to leave," Stanley said sharply. "I paid good money for this vacation, and I'm not going to leave early because of a few snowflakes. I mean, the whole point of this place is snow, right?"

"I guess," I said. "But a lot of people are worried about the storm, so I just thought—"

Once again, he cut me off. "Other people can do what

they want. I'm staying—and the lodge had just better make sure I get my money's worth one way or another." He glared at Mrs. Gallagher.

Mrs. Gallagher started talking calmly about the activities they had planned for the guests who were staying. I felt sorry for her, having to deal with a jerk like Stanley. Anyone witnessing that argument in the dining room the night before probably would have assumed the two participants shared equal blame, or might even have thought the bigger, stronger Nate was picking on wimpy little Stanley. But now I knew better. Nate seemed like a cool guy, while Stanley . . . not so much.

But that didn't matter right now. I was running out of time. I needed to find someone who was leaving soon, or it would be too late.

"Excuse me," I murmured. Mrs. Gallagher shot me a helpless, faintly amused look. Stanley didn't even seem to notice I was leaving.

I headed back into the lobby. Poppy Song was just coming in from the opposite direction.

"Hi, Frank!" she called when she spotted me. She hurried over with a smile. "Hey, does this mean you guys decided to stick around through the storm?"

"Not exactly." I quickly filled her in on the jalopy situation. "You didn't change your mind about leaving, did you?" I asked hopefully.

"Sorry." Poppy shrugged. "I don't have a car here anyway—

my friends took our rental when they left. One of the employees is supposed to drive me down to the airport in the lodge's van next week."

"Oh." My shoulders slumped. "Okay."

"Did you ask the owners if they could drive you out of here?" Poppy asked. "Like I said, they have a van for picking up guests who fly in. They advertise the service on their website, and everyone I've talked to who's used it says it's very convenient. I even heard they'll sometimes let guests reserve the van to go into town for dinner or other activities." She shrugged again. "Maybe someone could take you to town in it."

I felt a spark of hope. Then I spotted Mr. Gallagher rushing through the lobby, loaded down with suitcases. Rick was right behind him, toting a folded-up playpen and a large stuffed bear.

"That's okay," I said. "They're pretty busy right now. Besides, I think I see someone else I can ask."

With a quick good-bye to Poppy, I hurried to intercept Mrs. Richmond, the frazzled mother of the four little kids who'd been hanging all over Cody's dog earlier.

"Excuse me," I said. "Are you guys getting ready to leave?"

"That's the plan." Mrs. Richmond sighed, hoisting the wiggly toddler she was carrying higher on her hip. "It's taking a little longer than expected to pack everything up. I guess that's life with kids, right?" She smiled wearily.

"Mommy!" The toddler tugged on her hair. "Where's the doggie?"

"No more doggie," his mother said sternly. "We have to go."

"Um, listen," I said. "I have a question." I explained our situation.

She looked sympathetic. "Well, we won't have much space in the minivan, as you can probably guess." She glanced around at the other three kids, who were racing around, trying to hit one another with whatever toys, books, or mittens they were holding. "But you and your friends are welcome to try to cram yourselves into the back if you want." She cracked a wry smile. "Heck, if you guys can entertain these little monsters for a while, we'll take you wherever you want to go."

"Great!" Relief washed over me. "I'm sure we can fit. We only need a ride to the first decent-size town." I glanced at the kids. "And my brother's a pretty good storyteller, if that helps."

Mrs. Richmond chuckled and nodded. "My husband should be downstairs in a minute with the rest of our things. We'll meet you outside."

"Okay. Thanks a million!" I left her wrangling the kids and went in search of Joe and Chet. They weren't in the lobby, and when I went out to the portico, they weren't there, either. Mr. Gallagher was piling his latest load of luggage by the curb. "Have you seen my brother or Chet?" I asked him.

Rick heard me and looked up. "Those other two fellows from your group?" he asked in his gruff way. "They were heading out to the parking lot last I saw."

"Thanks." I guessed they'd gone out to tinker with the jalopy.

I headed out into the snow. As I did, I heard a sharp little bark. I was surprised—that definitely didn't sound like Blizzard, and I hadn't seen any other dogs on the property. A moment later, a tiny Chihuahua or something leaped into view through the rapidly increasing snowfall.

I say "or something" because if the thing hadn't just barked, I wouldn't have known it was a dog at all. It was dressed in a bright-pink coat that covered most of its body. A little knitted cap was tied around its head, covering everything except two big, dark eyes and a little pointy nose. The snow on the drive was already deep enough to come up to the tiny dog's chest, but it pranced high enough to show the matching pink booties on all four paws.

I was so busy taking in the dog's outfit that I didn't glance up until the person walking it greeted me by name. It was Josie. She was wrapped in a long parka and a hat with a pom-pom that matched her pet's coat.

"Hi," I greeted her. "I didn't know you had a dog."

Josie scooped up the tiny dog and cuddled it. "Oh, yes. Toy Toy is my sweetie pie," she said. "He's not usually supposed to be out around the guests, but I wanted to get him out for one last good walk before the blizzard hits. I figured it would be okay since almost everyone is gone." A shadow of anxiety passed over her face.

I didn't want to get into all that again. "Okay, have a nice walk," I said politely. "I'll see you later."

Or not. But like I said, I didn't want to get into that.

Joe and Chet were peering into the jalopy's engine when I reached them. "Did you figure out what's wrong?" I asked hopefully. Maybe we wouldn't be stuck entertaining four screaming kids all the way down the mountain after all.

"Nope," Joe said. "I don't think they've made most of these parts since, like, 1952."

"I'm sure I can figure it out eventually," Chet said. He shot me a sheepish look. "But she's not going to get us out of here today. Did you find us another ride?"

"Actually, I did." I told them about Mrs. Richmond's offer. "We're supposed to meet them out front in a few."

Joe actually looked a little disappointed. "And here I was just getting psyched to ride out the storm."

"Not me." I reached over and slammed the jalopy's hood shut. "Come on, we'd better go ask the Gallaghers if we can leave most of our luggage at the lodge and ship it home later. I have a feeling there's going to be very limited space in that minivan."

When we reached the portico, the Richmonds were nowhere in sight. "Uh-oh. Think they left without us?" Chet asked.

"Doubtful. I just talked to her a few minutes ago. They're probably still inside."

I led the way into the lobby. Sure enough, Mrs. Richmond was there, along with a tall, thin man I assumed was Mr. Richmond. They were talking to a worried-looking Mr. Gallagher as the kids ran around wildly.

We hurried over. "Boys," Mr. Gallagher said when he saw us. "I was just telling the Richmonds the latest news."

"What's that?" Joe asked.

"Rick just called the hotline to see if the roads are still safe." Mr. Gallagher gestured to the employee, who was stoking the fire nearby. "Apparently the wind has already picked up farther down the mountain. There are trees and power lines down all over the place, and the county just closed the main road."

"What?" Chet's face went pale. "So does that mean . . ."

"I'm afraid nobody else can leave," Mr. Gallagher said. "You'll have to stay here at the lodge through the storm."

6 BLIZZARD

JOE

"HEY BLIZZ—SIT!" I SWIPED A STRAY french fry from Frank's plate and held it up.

The dog's fuzzy ears perked up, and her long pink tongue flopped out. She sank down on her haunches, eyes trained on the fry.

"She's going to be totally spoiled." Cody smiled as I tossed the fry to his dog. "Mom and Dad don't normally let her in the dining room at mealtimes."

"Guess tonight's not exactly normal, huh?" Chet reached for his water glass.

No kidding. I scanned the dining room, which was almost empty. The Richmonds had just left to put their kids to bed, which immediately made the whole place a lot quieter. Only two tables besides ours were occupied. Nate and Cassie Katz were snuggled up together at one, probably feeding each other grapes or something. Stanley Wright was at another. Sitting by himself. Big surprise there.

Suddenly I noticed someone was missing. "Hey, what happened to Poppy?" I wondered. "She was sitting with the honeymooners a little while ago."

"She left right when I came in," Cody said, slipping Blizz a bit of hamburger that had fallen off Chet's plate. "Seemed like she was in a hurry—I said hi, but she rushed right past me."

"That doesn't sound like her." I reached for the salt-shaker. "Usually she's super chatty."

Chet grinned. "Why are you so interested in Poppy, Joe? Did you want to ask her to go for a moonlit walk through the blizzard with you?"

Frank chuckled and glanced at Cody, who looked slightly confused. "My brother likes to think he's a real ladies' man," Frank said.

"That's because it's true," I retorted. "Don't be a hater, bro."

"Isn't Poppy a little old for you?" Chet asked me. "She's got to be at least twenty-three."

I rolled my eyes. "You two are the ones claiming I'm interested in her, remember?"

"Yeah," Frank said. "Because she's the only attractive girl anywhere near our age around here."

"What about Josie?" Chet glanced at the waitress, who

had just hurried over to the honeymooners' table and was chatting and laughing with them. Luckily, her mood seemed to have improved since earlier. "She's attractive. And young."

"True." I shrugged. "She seems a little high-strung, though."

Cody checked his watch and stood up. "Listen, I just remembered—Mom asked me to take care of some stuff in the office tonight. Better go do it before I get in trouble. See you guys later." He whistled for Blizzard, and the two of them headed out.

"See you," Chet called after him. Then he grinned. "More dessert for us, right, guys?"

By the time we finished eating, the wind was howling outside. We wandered through the lobby and down the narrow hall leading to the back staircase, which led up to the end of the hall near our room. At the end of the downstairs hall we paused at the big picture window overlooking the path leading out to the ski shop and the slopes beyond. Huge floodlights lit the scene, though the snow was coming down so hard now that it blocked out some of the glow. Even so, it was easy to see that the storm was really raging. The wind rattled the windows and whipped the snow into tiny tornadoes that danced across the flat, open area between the lodge and the ski shop.

"Wow—cool," I murmured.

Frank shot me a look. "You're actually enjoying this, aren't you?"

"You mean being stranded here? Sure. It's an adventure. I'm kind of glad it worked out this way. Aren't you?"

He didn't respond, but I could read the answer on his face. That would be a big, fat NO. Sometimes I couldn't believe we were related.

Chet jumped back as the wind flung a twig against the window. "I'm just glad we're in here and not out there," he said with a shiver. Then he leaned forward and peered out the window. "Wait—is that someone out there?"

"Doubtful. Who'd be crazy enough to go out in this?" I said.

But Frank gasped. "He's right—there is someone out there!"

I could see it now too. A figure had just come into view near the ski shop. The poor visibility out there made it hard to tell anything other than it was a human, bundled up in bulky winter clothes and leaning forward against the wind.

"Who could that be?" I wondered. "Do you think we should go out there and try to help him?"

"I don't know." Frank bit his lip as the figure struggled a few steps forward across the open area. "Maybe we should get Mr. Gallagher."

But we all stood there watching as the figure kept moving slowly but steadily toward the lodge. "He's heading for the doors," Chet commented after a moment.

"Let's go let him in." Frank led the way to the big double doors leading out the side of the lodge toward the slopes.

Frank swung open the door and the figure rushed in, bringing a burst of snow and wind with him. It was Rick Ferguson. He peeled the scarf away from his face.

"Oh, hello, boys," he said. "Thanks for getting the door."

"Sure," I said, shoving the door shut. "What were you doing out there?"

Rick shrugged off his snow-covered parka. "Locking up the ski shack and other outbuildings," he said. "Wouldn't want the wind to blow open the doors overnight. Could be a real mess."

"Oh." I glanced at the door as it rattled in a gust of wind. "Seems like it's getting pretty bad out there."

"It is." Rick stepped over and yanked on the door handle, making sure the latch was secure. "You boys make sure to stay inside tonight, all right? Going to be too dangerous for man or beast out there soon." He tested the door once more, then nodded curtly. "Night, now."

"Good night," we chorused as Rick hurried off in the direction of the employees' quarters just down the hall.

Frank and Chet headed for the stairs, talking about who got first dibs in the shower. After one last look at the blizzard raging outside, I followed.

My heart pounded with terror as the giant monster truck's motor roared. It was coming right at me! I turned to run, but I knew it was too late. The motor roared again, sounding like a roar of triumph. . . .

I bolted upright, blinking in the darkness. Oh, right. Just a dream.

But the roaring sound wasn't my imagination. It was the

wind, howling around the lodge, making the whole building seem to tremble against its onslaught.

Stifling a yawn, I glanced at the table that separated my bed from Frank's. The clock's glowing green numbers were the only light in the room. Ten minutes after midnight.

Normally I had no trouble sleeping. I was a sleeping machine—day, night, car ride, English class, I could sleep right through any of them. But this was the third time the wind had awakened me tonight. I glanced at Frank, who was a motionless lump under the covers. Obviously the storm wasn't keeping him up. Or Chet, either, judging by the snoring coming from the suite's other bedroom.

Yawning again, I stood and stretched and headed for the window. I pulled back the curtains. Our suite had a fantastic view of the slopes, which meant it overlooked the courtyard where the ski shack and other outbuildings were located. The spotlights were still on down there, struggling to light the scene despite the windblown sheets of snow.

The storm was worse than ever. Deep drifts made the landscape look different than it had just a few hours earlier, climbing up the side of the ski shack and making everything look soft and uncertain. Ghostly wisps of blowing snow danced up and down the courtyard like whirling dervishes.

But wait—the snow wasn't the only thing moving out there. I pressed both hands against the cold glass of the window, getting as close as I could. Squinting as I tried to see through the blowing snow, I focused on a dark blob standing out against all that white.

"Is that a . . . person out there?" I whispered.

It couldn't be. Who would be crazy enough to wander out into a raging blizzard in the middle of the night?

Rick Ferguson, I thought. Maybe he was making sure he hadn't missed any of those doors. Or checking on the generator, which I was pretty sure was housed in one of the other outbuildings.

Or maybe this was another dream. Yeah, that was probably it. After all, it was pretty much a repeat of earlier that night, when the guys and I had spotted Rick through the picture window. Sort of like all those times I'd relived a particularly heinous social studies test or one of Mom's terrifying semiannual clothes-shopping expeditions the night after it had happened.

I stared down at the dark figure. It appeared to be moving away from the lodge. That was no biggie if this was a dream. If it wasn't?

Deciding I'd better figure it out one way or the other, I pinched my arm. Hard.

"Ow!" I yelped.

There was a muffled grunt from the direction of Frank's bed. A moment later he sat up, rubbing his eyes.

"Joe?" he mumbled, voice thick with sleep. "That you?"

"Yeah." I glanced at the figure outside. He was still moving away. In a moment, he'd be out of view behind the ski shack. "Get up—quick. There's someone outside!"

Not waiting for a response, I rushed next door and poked Chet in the shoulder. "Whu-huh?" he groaned.

"Up!" I was feeling more wide awake by the second. If my eyes weren't deceiving me, there was someone outside wandering deeper into the storm right now. If we didn't do something, there was no way he or she would last more than a few minutes out there.

I quickly pulled on my sneakers and explained what I'd seen as I led the others out of the suite and down the back stairwell. "Are you sure you saw a person?" Chet asked with a yawn. "I mean, who'd be crazy enough to go out in this?"

"I don't know. But I know what I saw." I put on a burst of speed as the side doors came into view.

"Maybe it was a bear," Frank mumbled.

"Even bears don't go out in this kind of weather. Plus, don't they hibernate during the winter anyway?" I hurried over to the door.

"Hey! What's going on out here?"

It was Rick. He'd just emerged from a doorway down the hall, dressed in jeans, a sweatshirt, and weathered suede slippers.

"There's someone outside." I reached for the door, but it wouldn't budge. It was locked! I moved to unlock it.

"What? Stop!" Rick hurried toward us, looking alarmed. "Don't open that—"

WHOOOSH!

I swung open the door, letting in a maelstrom of wind

and snow. Who said snowflakes are soft and pretty? They sure don't feel that way when they hit your face at a zillion miles an hour.

Shading my eyes, I took a step out. "Hello?" I called, my words whipped away instantly by the wind. "Anyone out there?"

"See anything?" As he joined me in the doorway, Frank sounded a little more awake. An instant forty-degree temperature drop will do that.

"No." I glanced at the ground. "I can't even tell if anyone came out this way. The wind would've blown away any prints."

"What are you guys thinking?" Rick sounded gruffer and crankier than ever as he rushed up and tried to wrestle the door out of my hand. "We've got to get this shut."

"No, wait!" I faced him. "I saw someone out there from my window—I swear! We have to check. If we don't . . ."

I let my voice trail off. Rick hesitated, looking annoyed. Then he sighed. When he spoke again, he sounded a little less gruff.

"Well, what are we supposed to do?" he said, glancing outside. "If we go out there right now, we could all die."

He had a point. I wasn't much in the mood for dying at the moment.

Suddenly I had an idea. "Wait right here," I told the others. "I'll be right back."

I hurried down the hallway, passing Rick's open door.

Just beyond was Cody's room. I knew where it was because we'd stopped by when we first arrived.

"Cody!" I pounded on the door. "Wake up! Emergency!"

Inside the room, Blizzard started barking immediately. After a moment, the door opened and a sleepy-looking Cody peered out.

"Joe?" he said. "What is it?"

Blizzard pushed past him, jumping out into the hallway, her ears and tail on alert. "I need Blizz." I pointed at the dog. "You mentioned at dinner the other night that she's an excellent tracker, right? Like, she finds people who are lost in the snow."

Cody blinked at me. "In theory, yeah. We've only trained for it, though; she's never been tested in a real-life situation. Why?"

I told him about the person I'd seen outside. By the time I finished, Cody looked more awake.

"Okay, we can try, I guess." He sounded a little dubious. "But if it's too bad out there, we're coming right back. Let me just grab my boots and jacket."

As he disappeared back into his room, Frank came over to pat Blizz. "Do you think this will work?" he asked.

I shrugged. "We'll find out."

Soon Cody was clipping a leash onto Blizz's collar, and the two of them were diving out into the storm. We swung the door mostly shut to keep the snow out, leaving only a crack so we could watch for them to return.

"I don't know about this," Rick muttered. "I should wake up Cody's parents and let them know what's happening."

But he didn't move, watching that crack in the door along with the rest of us. My heart was pounding. Would this work? Or would we end up having to figure out a way to rescue the rescuers?

The seconds passed slowly, each one feeling more like an hour. "How long should we give them?" Chet asked at last.

"Don't know." Rick checked his watch. "If they don't come back soon—"

"Look!" Frank interrupted. "Is that them?"

We all leaned forward. A dark blob was just visible beyond the walls of snow. A moment later part of the blob broke free and bounded forward—it was Blizz, leaping through the drifts as she raced toward the door, barking.

"Help!" Cody's voice came, barely audible over the wind. "I can't drag him much farther!"

"Come on!" I rushed outside, barely noticing the cold wind ripping through my clothes or the snow soaking through my sneakers. Frank and Rick were right behind me.

It was hard going through the storm, but finally we reached Cody. A man was leaning heavily on him as he stumbled through the snow.

"Got him!" Frank said, slinging the guy's other arm over his shoulder.

Working together, he and Cody rushed the man toward

the door. I led the way, shouting for Chet to open wide. Blizz raced back and forth, barking.

It was only when we were all safely inside, with Rick shoving the door shut, that we all got a good look at the guy we'd just rescued.

My mouth dropped open as I recognized him.

"Stanley!" I blurted out.

7

CLOSE CALL

FRANK

JOE SOUNDED STUNNED AS HE SAID Stanley's name. I knew how he felt.

Stanley's teeth were chattering, and his face was very pale. He had to be at least half-frozen despite his coat and hat.

"Are you all right?" I asked him.

"What were you doing out there?" Rick demanded at the same time.

"You okay, dude?" Chet asked Cody, who nodded. Blizzard shook the snow off her thick coat and then danced around all of us, letting out an occasional bark.

Meanwhile doors were opening up and down the hall as the commotion woke people. Mr. and Mrs. Gallagher were among the first to arrive.

"What's going on out here?" Mrs. Gallagher asked, tying her robe shut as she hurried over to Cody. Then she saw Stanley and gasped. "Oh, my! What happened to you?"

Stanley's teeth were still chattering, but his face was already returning to its normal sallow shade. "I could have f-f-frozen to d-d-death!" he exclaimed. "I've b-b-been locked out there for hours!"

A gasp went up from the people gathered around us. Mrs. Gallagher rushed back into her room and returned with a blanket, which she threw around Stanley.

Meanwhile Blizzard perked up her ears and bounded down the hall, wagging her tail. Josie had just emerged from her room with her little dog clutched in her arms. As I watched the big dog and little dog touch noses, I realized Toy Toy wasn't a Chihuahua after all—he was a poodle. But I wasn't too concerned about that at the moment.

"Oh, you poor man!" The lodge's head chef, a heavyset woman with a beet-red face, stared at Stanley. "You must be absolutely frozen!"

"Yes. But how did you get outside in the first place?" Mr. Gallagher sounded confused.

Stanley turned to glare at Josie. "I only intended to step outside for a moment," he said. "Someone failed to empty the wastebasket in my room, and I couldn't sleep from the smell of my old banana peel rotting away in there. I fig-

ured there had to be a Dumpster out there somewhere."
He waved a hand in the vague direction of the door. "But
I couldn't find one, and when I tried to come back in, the
door was locked!"

"Oh, dear," someone said.

I glanced around. It was Mrs. Richmond. She and her
husband had just emerged from the back stairwell, both of
them wrapped in fluffy white robes with the Granite Peak
Lodge logo on them. Clearly the noise had carried from the
employees' quarters up to at least some of the second-floor
guest rooms.

"The door must lock automatically, eh?" Nate Katz spoke
up. He was right behind the Richmonds, dressed in sweat-
pants, a T-shirt, and bare feet, though his wife was nowhere
in sight.

Rick frowned. "No," he said. "This door doesn't do that—
it's an emergency exit. It can only be locked with a key."

"Who has the key?" I asked.

Rick shrugged. "We all do. There's a master key that
works most of the door locks around here."

"That's right. Everyone who works here has a copy of the
key," Mr. Gallagher confirmed, turning to his staff. "So did
any of you lock this door tonight?"

All the employees present shook their heads. Stanley
frowned. "Well, I got locked out there somehow," he insisted,
letting out a sudden shiver.

Mrs. Gallagher tut-tutted. "Enough talking," she said,

putting an arm around Stanley. "Let's get you to the infirmary."

As she bustled him off down the hall, Stanley was still complaining. Mr. Gallagher sighed and rubbed his beard as he watched them go. There was a worried crease in his forehead, and I could guess what he was thinking. Why did this have to happen to Stanley Wright of all people?

"All right, everyone," Mr. Gallagher said. "Go on back to bed. We'll take care of this and update everyone in the morning."

People started drifting back toward their rooms. I stepped over to Cody. "Nice work out there, you two," I said, patting Blizzard on the head. "Stanley might not seem very grateful right now, but I'm sure he'll realize he owes you his life."

"I wouldn't have even known he was out there if you guys hadn't sounded the alarm," Cody said. "Anyway, Blizz is the one who found him."

"Yeah." I shot Joe a proud glance. He might seem like kind of a spaz most of the time, but once in a while my brother really comes through. "That was good thinking, running for Blizz."

"I'm just glad she was here." Joe shrugged modestly. "Come on, might as well try to get some sleep."

But when he, Chet, and I reached our suite, none of us were feeling sleepy. We sprawled on Chet's bed, talking about what had just happened.

"It must have been an accident, right?" Chet said.

Joe shrugged. "Rick said that door shouldn't lock unless someone locks it," he reminded us.

"Yeah." I'd been thinking about that. "He was awfully quick to speak up about it, actually."

"What are you saying?" Joe raised one eyebrow. "You think Rick locked Stanley out there?"

"Not on purpose." I picked at a loose thread on the bedspread. "I imagine it was an honest mistake. He was awfully worried about doors blowing open earlier, remember? He might've locked that one just in case the wind picked up even more."

"So why didn't he say so?" Chet wondered.

"Maybe he was afraid he'd be blamed—might be afraid of losing his job over it or something." I chewed my lower lip, thinking it over. "We don't know anything about him or his history here, after all."

Chet looked troubled. "Then again, maybe it wasn't an accident," he said. "Did you guys notice that Rick was still dressed just now?"

Come to think of it, I had. "So what?" I said. "It's not that late. Some people are night owls. Or maybe he was supposed to stay up and keep an eye on things tonight because of the storm."

"Maybe," Joe said. "Still, if we were investigating this incident—and I'm not saying we are—I'd probably have to put Mr. Rick Ferguson on the suspect list."

"I'd put Stanley on it too," Chet said. "It's pretty weird how all the mysterious stuff happens to him, right? Besides, the guy is just a jerk, and he complains about everything."

Joe grinned. "You think he locked himself out in the snow to die? Yeah, that would give him something to complain about, all right."

"Whatever." I stifled a yawn, still turning everything that had happened over in my head. "For all we know, it could've been Josie who locked him out there."

"Josie?" Chet echoed. "How do you figure?"

"I'm just kidding, mostly," I said. "It's just that she seems really worried about losing her job. Maybe she thought all of Stanley's complaining would make business even worse. Or something."

Joe snorted. "Bro, I think your brain's already asleep, even if the rest of you isn't."

"Sleep." Chet rolled over and yawned. "Yeah, that's starting to sound good."

I had to agree. "Come on, Joe, let's go back to our room." Chet's yawn was contagious, and my mouth stretched open so wide I was afraid my head would crack in two. "We can worry about all this in the morning."

In the morning the storm was still going strong. The wind battered the windows, swirling the snow around so much it was impossible to see more than a few feet. But the lodge was warm and cozy. Joe, Chet, and I got dressed and followed the enticing scents of coffee and bacon to the dining room.

The Richmonds were sitting over near the kitchen door, making a racket as usual. The honeymooners were at a table for two near the entrance. They smiled at us as we passed before going back to making moony eyes at each other.

Poppy was sitting by herself nearby, sipping coffee and typing on a laptop. When she spotted us, she shut the computer and waved us over.

"So what happened last night?" she demanded before we could say a word. "I can't believe I slept through the whole thing!"

Joe flopped into a chair and reached for the coffeepot in the middle of the table. "What have you heard so far?"

"Not much," she said. "I just got here. But one of the Richmond kids said someone almost got turned into a snowman last night, and the dog rescued him?" She grinned. "What's the real story?"

The honeymooners heard her and looked up, and Nate leaned closer. "That's pretty much it, actually. Stanley Wright accidentally locked himself out in the blizzard, and by the time Cody's dog tracked him down, he was half-frozen. Couldn't have happened to a more deserving guy."

"Nate!" his wife exclaimed, sounding horrified.

"Sorry." Shooting us a sheepish look, Nate returned his attention to his own table.

"Wow." Poppy turned to us. "Is all that true?"

"Yeah," Joe said. "I happened to wake up around midnight and spotted Stanley through the window." He shrugged. "Well, I didn't know it was him at the time. But we ran down and got Cody and Blizz to get out there and take a look, and the rest is history."

Poppy looked impressed, and I could tell Joe was eating it up. "I can't believe I missed the whole thing," she said. "Sounds like I was the only one. I'm a pretty sound sleeper." She leaned forward. "So was Stanley okay? How'd the Gallaghers react when they found out?"

"He seemed okay to me," Chet said. "We haven't seen him since—"

"Excuse me," Poppy said suddenly, cutting him off. "I just remembered I, um, have to go. Sorry."

She leaped to her feet, grabbed her laptop, and raced away, disappearing through the door leading into the side hallway, where the lodge's small gift shop, public restrooms, and various other amenities were located. I stared after her in surprise.

"That was weird," I said.

Chet shrugged. "Maybe she really, really felt like shopping. Or needed to use the bathroom."

Joe rolled his eyes. "You really don't know anything about girls, do you, dude?"

"Never mind that." I'd just noticed Josie rushing toward us, Toy Toy clutched in her arms. She must have come in from the lobby while we were focused on Poppy's departure.

"Have you guys seen Stanley?" Josie blurted out. "He hasn't shown up here, has he?"

Joe shrugged. "Not that we know of. But we just got here ourselves."

"Why? Is everything okay?" I asked.

"I just want to make sure he's all right." Josie bit her lip, looking anxious. "You know—after last night. I'm sure he's very upset."

Nate leaned over again from his table. "Are you talking about Stanley? I saw him a few minutes ago out in the lobby, complaining to Mr. Gallagher about something." He rolled his eyes. "In other words, he seems to be back to his usual self."

Joe let out a snort of laughter, and Chet grinned. But Cassie gave her husband a disapproving poke in the shoulder, and Josie just frowned.

Meanwhile, I tried to add cream to my coffee and discovered the pitcher was empty. "Be right back," I said, standing up. Yeah, I could have asked Josie to go get me some. But she seemed a little distracted right now. Besides, she already had enough to do—there only seemed to be maybe half a dozen employees left on the property other than the Gallaghers.

On the way to the kitchen, I passed the Richmonds' table. One of the kids appeared to be having a meltdown.

"I didn't lose them!" the little boy was insisting, his face bright red as he glared at his parents. "I left them by the fire to dry, and someone stealed them!"

"You mean stole them." Mrs. Gallagher sighed. "And nobody stole your boots, kiddo. I promise. Who would do that?"

I paused by the table. "Lost boots, huh?" I said with a friendly smile. I hadn't forgotten that the Richmonds had been willing to let us cram into their already crowded van. That made me like them. "I'll keep an eye out for them, buddy. What do they look like?"

"They're red." The little boy gave me a slightly suspicious look. "And they didn't get lost. They got stoleden!"

I chuckled and traded an amused look with the boy's parents. "Well, maybe you can ask the Gallaghers to make an announcement," I suggested. "I'm sure they'll be able to help you solve the mystery."

"Thanks." Mr. Richmond smiled and winked. "We'll do that."

I moved on to the coffee station outside the kitchen. I turned back toward the table just in time to see Stanley march into the dining room. He didn't look happy.

"Be careful, everyone," he announced loudly. "Don't go anywhere alone unless you want what happened to me to happen to you, too." He scowled and shook his fist. "This place is a deathtrap!"

BREAKING THE RULES

8

JOE

ROLLED MY EYES AT STANLEY'S MELODRA-matic announcement. But Frank was frowning as he returned to our table, and Chet looked worried.

"What a jerk," Chet said as Mrs. Gallagher appeared and started talking soothingly to Stanley while steering him toward the coffee station.

"Yeah, he's a charmer all right." Frank sat down and poured milk into his coffee. "I wouldn't pay any attention to him."

Chet still looked upset. "Maybe you wouldn't, but what if other people do? One jerk like Stanley could be all it takes to ruin the Gallaghers' business!"

I was about to say that Chet was crazy to worry about that. Then I remembered something.

"Josie made it sound like this place is in more serious financial trouble than we realized," I mused.

"Hmm, I suppose you're right," Frank said. "In which case, maybe Chet's got a point. The last thing the Gallaghers need is for Stanley to start spreading rumors all over the Internet about this place."

Chet looked troubled. "Are they really rumors, though? He did almost freeze out there last night."

"And he could have been injured on that mismarked ski trail the other day," I added. "Face it, some weird stuff has happened to Stanley Wright here."

"I know." Chet bit his lip, looking from me to Frank and back again. "That's why . . ." He hesitated.

Frank sipped his coffee. "What?"

"What if it's not just bad luck?" Chet leaned forward. "What if someone at the lodge is out to get Stanley?" He shot a slightly nervous look over at Nate, who was paying no attention to us whatsoever as he stared deeply into Cassie's eyes. Not that I blamed him. If I was married to a woman like that, I'd never look at anything else either.

But never mind that. "So what are you saying?" I asked Chet.

"I'm saying maybe you guys could look into it—just in case." He stared at us hopefully. "Please?"

"You mean, like, investigate?" I said.

"Whoa," Frank said at the same time. "We're trying to stay away from that kind of thing, remember?"

"I know. But I won't tell." Chet sighed. "I just want to help Cody if I can. He's hiding it pretty well, but I can tell he's really worried about this place."

I glanced at Frank. "What do you think, bro? Couldn't hurt to check it out. It's not like we have much else to do until the weather clears."

"I guess so," Frank agreed slowly.

Chet grinned with relief. "Thanks, you guys! Come on, let's go somewhere more private and figure out how to get started."

"Okay." I stood and grabbed my coffee. "But only if we can swing by the buffet table on the way. I need some food for thought."

It was surprisingly difficult to find a private spot in the lodge. Mr. Gallagher was in the lobby, one of the maids was vacuuming the carpet in the hallway near the side door, and Poppy was poking around in the magazine racks in the library alcove near the gift shop.

Finally we settled in the small lounge that contained the lodge's indoor hot tub. We had a great view of the storm from there through the wall of windows overlooking the bunny slope. Not that we could see the bunny slope. Snow was coming down so fast the whole scene looked like one of those modern art paintings that's all one color. In this case, white.

"Wow." Chet peered out. "We're not getting out of here anytime soon, are we?"

Frank sat down and took a bite of the bagel he'd grabbed

from the buffet. "It'll probably be another twenty-four hours at least."

"That gives us plenty of time to solve the mystery." Chet sank onto the leather couch.

"If there even is a mystery here," I said. "Well, other than the mystery of how much bad luck one dude can have in a week."

"Yeah. But it's not too hard to imagine someone might have it out for Stanley, right?" Chet said.

Frank shrugged. "True. He's pretty rude. I can't imagine he's a favorite of the staff by this point."

"Or anyone else, either." I stared at my bacon-and-egg biscuit, thinking back to Stanley's confrontation with Nate. "Just about everyone at the lodge probably wishes he'd go away—staff and other guests alike."

"But is that enough of a motive for anyone to actually try to kill him?" Frank said. "Taking down the closed sign on that ski trail was dangerous. But locking Stanley out in the storm last night? I'd have to call that attempted murder."

"Yeah, that was pretty hardcore," I agreed. "Then again, we really don't know much about most of the people here. Who knows what they're capable of?"

Chet looked nervous. "You think someone here is, like, a hardened criminal or something?"

"How would we know?" Frank stirred his coffee. "We've busted some pretty normal-seeming people over the years who turned out to be totally heinous."

"Yeah."

I glanced at Frank. He had that look in his eye. The look that meant his logical little mind was working.

"We've got one advantage here," he said. "A limited number of possible suspects. The incident last night happened after most of the guests and staff had left. If we assume the same person was responsible for the trail sign incident . . ."

"Our culprit has to be someone who's still here now," I finished. "Okay, so who've we got?"

"What about Nate?" Chet suggested immediately. "He looked like he wanted to punch Stanley's lights out at dinner the other night."

Frank nodded. "Nate seems like a nice enough guy, but he clearly doesn't like Stanley. He should go on the list."

"Then there's Rick Ferguson," I said. "Like we were saying last night, it's a little strange that he was still dressed after midnight. There could be a perfectly innocent reason, but—"

Chet's eyes widened. "He tried to stop us from opening the door, remember?" he blurted out. "What if that's because he's the one who locked Stanley out there? He does kind of seem like a tough guy." He cast a nervous look around the lounge, as if fearing that Rick could appear out of nowhere and toss him out the window.

"Okay, so we've got Nate and Rick," Frank said. "Who else?"

I gulped down a bite of my sandwich. "What about

Poppy? She was acting weird just now. And she's practically the only one who didn't hear Blizz barking last night and come out to see what was happening. What if it's because she didn't want everyone to see her looking guilty?"

Frank looked skeptical. "The Richmond kids didn't come out either. Should they go on the list too?"

"Maybe." I was only half-kidding. "But seriously, it's kind of strange that Poppy stayed behind at the lodge when all her friends left."

"She said her apartment's being fumigated." Frank looked distracted. "Speaking of the Richmond kids . . ."

"What?" I said. "You think they're a gang of mini murderers?"

"No, it's not that. But one of the boys was complaining about his boots being stolen." Frank shrugged, looking slightly sheepish. "I know it's probably not connected, but . . ."

"You never know," I said with a grin. "Maybe someone's going to try to frame poor Stanley for the theft."

"You never know," Frank echoed, grinning back.

I could tell he was enjoying this. So was I.

Chet was picking at his food, not looking like he was having quite such a good time. "Maybe we could try to check out some of these people online," he said.

"We could, if the storm hasn't knocked out the phone lines," Frank said dubiously, glancing out at the wind-whipped snow.

"Yeah." I wasn't holding my breath. There was no high-speed Internet access at the lodge—dial-up only. Yet another reason people were flocking to those other resorts, according to Cody.

Frank popped the last bit of bagel in his mouth. "Well, can't hurt to check," he said. "I'll run to the office and try the computer while you two start talking to people and sniffing around for clues."

"Sounds like a plan." I wolfed down the last few bites of my sandwich and wiped off the grease on my pants. "Chet, you want to talk to Nate or Rick?"

"Um, neither?" Chet looked nervous. "You guys are the experts at this. How about if I go check on the Internet situation while you two do the questioning?"

I traded an amused look with Frank. "Sure thing," I said. "I'll take Nate."

Frank nodded. "Then Rick's mine. Let's go."

I headed back toward the dining room. Before I got there, I spotted Nate and Cassie emerging into the lobby. That was easy.

"Hey, guys," I said, hurrying over. "Listen, Nate, I wanted to ask you something."

"Sure thing." Nate smiled. His arm was around Cassie's shoulders, and he looked relaxed and happy. "Ask away."

"It's about your little tiff with Stanley Wright at dinner the other night . . . ," I began.

Suddenly Nate's whole demeanor changed. His face went tight and grim, and his body stiffened.

"Cassie, sweetie," he said loudly, cutting me off. "I think I left my camera somewhere. Would you mind checking in the dining room? I'll run upstairs and see if it's in our room."

Cassie looked slightly surprised, but she nodded. "Of course. Meet you back here in a few?"

"Absolutely. Thanks, babe." He dropped a quick kiss on her cheek.

As Cassie headed back into the dining room, Nate grabbed my arm and dragged me toward the stairs. "Come with me," he whispered loudly.

"Okay." Not that I had much choice. The dude was apparently just as strong as he looked, judging by his iron grip.

Soon we were in the upstairs hallway. Nate cast a cautious look around, but there was nobody in sight.

"Listen," he said, his voice low and urgent. "About Stanley . . ."

I held my breath. Was he about to confess?

"Yeah?" I said. "What about him?"

Nate sighed and rubbed one meaty hand over his face. "Look, sorry for yanking you up here like that. It's just that I really don't want Cassie to know I went off on that jerk Stanley at dinner the other night. She's always after me about my temper, and I know better than to let a guy like that push my buttons, you know?"

"Okay," I said, a little confused. "Um, so what did he say to you that night, anyway?"

"He was complaining about this place." Nate waved a hand to indicate the lodge. "He was being pretty rude about it, saying he didn't know why anyone would want to come to a dump like this."

I shrugged. "Sounds like Stanley."

Nate nodded. "But see, Cassie's the one who wanted to honeymoon here, so I took it as an insult to her. Guess I was a little too sensitive, huh?" He actually cracked a smile. "It's a lot easier to ignore Stanley now that I've realized he complains about everything."

"Yeah."

Nate glanced at his watch. "Anyway, I should get back to Cass," he said. "We're scheduled to attend that wildlife lecture Mr. Gallagher is giving this morning. You going?"

"Um, I don't think so. But have fun." I vaguely recalled seeing a sign in the lobby about the lecture. The Gallaghers had scheduled several different indoor activities today. Probably trying to keep their snowbound guests from going stir-crazy.

Nate hurried for the stairs. I turned the opposite way, heading for my suite. I was pretty sure I'd stuck a notebook and pen in my bag. Might as well grab them in case I needed to jot down notes about the case.

When I emerged from the suite, I headed for the back stairwell nearby. I might as well go down that way—it was closer, plus it would give me a chance to take a look around near the scene of last night's rescue.

As soon as I opened the stairwell door, a blast of cold air hit me. That was weird, since the rest of the lodge was toasty warm.

Or maybe not so weird. There was a window on the landing halfway down, and I could see that it was wide open. Had the wind done it? I had no clue, but I hurried down the first flight of steps and shut it. I'd have to mention it to the Gallaghers the next time I saw them.

I started down the second flight at a jog, my shoes clattering on the metal steps. Less than halfway down, my feet suddenly shot out from under me.

"Whoa!" I yelled as I felt myself falling.

TOO SLICK

9

FRANK

AFTER PARTING WAYS WITH JOE AND Chet, I'd started looking for Rick. A few minutes later I still hadn't found him, but I ran into Mr. Richmond in the hall leading toward the kids' playroom, which was located near the side door across from the employees' quarters.

"Find your son's boots yet?" I asked with a smile.

He chuckled. "Not yet. I'm sure he left them somewhere and forgot where. He's always misplacing his toys, and—"

He was interrupted by a faint shout. It sounded frantic and echoey—and kind of familiar.

"Is that Joe?" I muttered. "But where . . ."

Not bothering to finish the question, I rushed down the

hall. Spotting the door leading to the back stairwell, I flung it open.

"Frank!" Joe shouted.

"Joe!" I took a step inside the stairwell and skidded. Glancing down, I saw a gleaming puddle on the concrete floor. No, not a puddle—a patch of ice.

"Careful, there's ice in here!" Joe called. "On the stairs, too!"

He was clinging to the metal railing embedded in the wall about halfway up. His feet were slipping and sliding on the steps. I gulped as I realized what must have happened. Joe, in a hurry as always, had hit a patch of ice on the stairs. If he hadn't grabbed the railing in time to stop himself, he would have gone flying down the rest of the way.

Mr. Richmond peered into the stairwell behind me and caught on right away. "Oh no! Hang on there, buddy. I'll get help." He took off in the direction of the lobby.

Meanwhile I stepped forward, being careful to avoid the ice on the floor. "Easy, bro," I said. "Just hang on."

"No, I'm okay." Joe started lowering himself carefully, hand by hand, along the railing. "Stay right there to break my fall just in case, okay?"

I rolled my eyes. Then I held my breath as I watched him make his way down like an oversize spider monkey. As he reached the bottom step, I heard footsteps coming.

"Careful, there's ice in here," I said, stepping into the

doorway. Mr. Richmond was back, accompanied by Mr. Gallagher, Chet, Nate and Cassie, and Josie, who was clutching her tiny dog.

"Ice?" Mr. Gallagher said. He pushed past me and looked around. "How'd that happen?"

"Don't know." Joe carefully lowered himself to the floor, picking his way to the safety of the carpeted hallway. "It goes almost up to the landing, though."

Chet shivered and wrapped his arms around himself. "Why's it so cold in there?"

"The window was open," Joe said. "I closed it on my way down." He shot me a look, and I guessed what he was thinking. If someone had done this on purpose, Joe had accidentally messed up any fingerprints that might have been on the window.

"Good thing you didn't slip down the stairs and crack your head open, Joe," Nate commented.

"He almost did," I said grimly.

"Yeah," Joe said. "I grabbed the railing just in time."

"Are you all right, Joe?" Mr. Gallagher asked. Without waiting for an answer, he turned to Josie. "Get Rick—ask him to block the doors until we get this cleaned up."

Josie didn't respond. She was staring wide-eyed at Joe. "Oh my gosh," she exclaimed. "You could have been killed! How could something like this happen?"

"It's all right, Josie," Cassie spoke up soothingly, putting a hand on Josie's arm. "He's okay. See?"

"But what if he wasn't?" Josie squeezed Toy Toy so tightly that the little dog squeaked and wiggled. "What if he'd fallen and hurt himself? It's just too much!"

She was getting so worked up I was afraid she might hyperventilate.

"I'll go look for Rick," I told Mr. Gallagher. After all, I wanted to talk to the guy anyway. "Any idea where he might be?"

Mr. Gallagher was still staring at the icy stairwell, looking troubled. "Saw him last over by the main stairs."

I nodded and looked at Joe. "Coming?"

"Right behind you," Joe replied. He gestured for Chet to stick with the others. Good idea. He could let us know what they said.

Joe and I found Rick in the lobby near the main staircase. He was talking with Poppy, who looked worried.

". . . and I'm pretty sure I left it on the bench by the picture window," she was saying. "But when I remembered and went to get it, it wasn't there."

"Something missing?" Joe asked.

Poppy nodded. "My MP3 player."

"Bummer," I said. Then I turned to Rick. "Mr. Gallagher needs you."

The man's face was always kind of grim, but it went grimmer as I told him what had happened.

"Just what we need," he muttered. "I'll take care of it. Better block the upstairs door first."

He rushed up the stairs, taking them three at a time. Joe and I followed.

"The upper flight of steps seemed okay," Joe told the man as we hurried down the upstairs hallway. "You should be able to get a look from the landing."

I was barely listening. I'd just spotted someone reaching for the door of the back stairwell. Stanley!

"Stop!" I called. "Stanley, don't go in there!"

"Huh?" Stanley turned to stare as we raced up to him.

"This stairwell's off-limits right now," Rick said. "You can use the main stairwell instead."

Stanley frowned, looking stubborn. "But this one's closer to my room," he said. "Why's it closed?"

"Ice on the stairs," I said, figuring it was better to be straight with him. All we needed was for Stanley to have yet another accident.

"Yeah," Joe confirmed. "I almost wiped out just now."

"What?" Stanley sounded horrified. "This is outrageous! I take these stairs all the time—I could have been killed! Again!"

He glared around at all three of us, as if holding us personally responsible. Then he took off toward the other stairs, muttering angrily under his breath.

Joe winced. "Just what the Gallaghers need."

"Exactly what I was thinking." I glanced at Rick. "You need our help?"

Rick shook his head, reaching for the door. "Got it covered. Thanks."

Joe and I took off after Stanley. When we got downstairs, he was ranting and raving at Mr. and Mrs. Gallagher, who were in the lobby with Chet, Nate and Cassie, and the Richmonds. Josie was perched on an overstuffed sofa nearby, hugging her little dog and looking anxious.

". . . and I'm starting to think someone's trying to kill me!" Stanley was exclaiming. "There was the situation last night, and of course the problem on the slopes the other day—"

"Wait, what problem on the slopes?" Mrs. Gallagher broke in.

Stanley looked surprised. "Didn't your son tell you? I could have been badly injured!"

As he dramatically described the incident, making it sound even worse than it was, Mrs. Gallagher gave her husband a worried look. I was surprised. Hadn't he told her about the missing CLOSED sign?

A moment later Rick came down the main stairs. He hurried over and whispered something in Mr. Gallagher's ear.

Mr. Gallagher's expression went even darker, if possible. "The back stairwell is closed until further notice," he announced to the lobby at large. He cleared his throat nervously. "I'd also like to let you all know that several items have gone missing since the storm started."

Several? I traded a surprised look with Joe.

"What kind of items?" Chet asked.

"Small things, mostly," Mr. Gallagher replied. "A child's snow boots, a pair of sunglasses, a hat, and now a guest's MP3 player."

"Oh, dear," Cassie said, huddling closer to Nate. "Is there a thief in our midst?"

"I expect it's just a prank." Mr. Gallagher's gaze wandered briefly toward the Richmond kids, who were arguing over a toy near the fireplace, completely oblivious to the adult conversation. "Just be careful, all right?"

"What about that ice on the steps?" Stanley demanded. "Do you think that's a prank too? Because I could have been killed!"

Mr. Gallagher bit his lip. "We're looking into that incident," he said shortly. "We'll keep you all posted."

"Not good enough." Stanley glared at him. "If you don't do something about this, sir, I might have to—"

"Wait!" Josie interrupted, jumping up from her seat on the sofa. "Stop, please. Don't blame the Gallaghers." She took a deep breath as a tear leaked out of one eye. "It was me—I did it. I did it all!"

CONFESSION 10

JOE

MY JAW DROPPED. FRANK AND CHET looked just as stunned at Josie's confession.

"You what?" Mrs. Gallagher blurted out. "Josie, what are you talking about?"

"I did it all," Josie insisted. The tears were flowing freely now. "I took away the sign on the closed slope by mistake, and I locked that door last night after I took Toy Toy for a walk." She bit her lip, glancing at Stanley. "I also spilled the water in the stairwell when I was mopping in there earlier. I meant to clean it up, but I got busy and forgot. Then the window must have blown open, and it froze."

"What about the missing MP3 player and other stuff?" Frank asked.

Josie shrugged, looking briefly uncertain. "I probably moved all that stuff accidentally while I was cleaning. I'm sure I can find everything if you give me a chance to search."

Mrs. Gallagher took her firmly by the arm. "Come with me," she said sternly. "We'd better go have a talk in the office."

Mr. Gallagher nodded, still looking worried. "All right, everything's under control," he said.

"But—" Stanley began.

Mr. Gallagher cut him off with a stern look. "It's time for our wildlife lecture," he said. "Anyone who's interested in attending, please follow me to the lounge and we'll get started."

The other guests were still murmuring and looking concerned. But the newlyweds followed Mr. Gallagher out of the lobby, along with Stanley and the whole Richmond family. Rick hurried off in the direction of the icy stairwell, leaving me, Frank, and Chet alone in the lobby.

"Wow, that wasn't exactly how I was expecting this case to end," Frank commented, wandering over to the fireplace.

"No kidding," I said.

"At least it's over." Chet sounded relieved. "Now Stanley will have no more excuses to bad-mouth the lodge, and things can get back to normal."

I glanced at the window. "As normal as possible during the blizzard of the century, anyway."

Frank stared into the crackling flames. I could tell something was bugging him.

"Josie said she was out walking Toy Toy last night." He seemed to be talking as much to himself as to Chet and me. "But yesterday afternoon she told me she was taking him for his last walk before the blizzard set in."

"So what?" I shrugged. "Dogs have to go when they have to go."

"Yeah. But a dog that size probably doesn't have to go outside," Frank said. "That's what puppy pads are made for, right? And Josie seems pretty protective of Toy Toy. Can you seriously picture her taking him out into the middle of a raging blizzard?"

"Who knows? Who cares?" Chet said. "She confessed, remember?"

"I know, but . . ." Frank's voice trailed off uncertainly.

I grinned. "I get it, dude." I clapped Frank on the back. "I'm a little bummed too. Who knew this mystery would get wrapped up so fast?"

"It's not that," he said quickly.

"Sure it is." I flopped onto a chair. "We're all a little bored being stuck inside. But this is one mystery that's already solved."

"I guess you're right," Frank muttered, though he didn't look happy about it.

Time to distract him. "Hey, there's a Ping-Pong table in the kids' playroom," I said, jumping to my feet. "And all those little Richmonds are at the wildlife lecture, so we'd have the place to ourselves. Who's up for a game or three?"

Soon Frank and I were hitting the little white ball back and forth. Chet lounged in an undersized plastic kids' chair on the sidelines, cheering and giving us advice on our technique.

"Score!" I crowed as I hit the ball right past Frank's paddle.

He barely noticed. He was staring past me into the hall outside. "There's Cody," he said. "He doesn't look happy."

Chet jumped up. "Cody!" he called through the doorway. "What's up? Haven't seen you in a while—where've you been?"

"Yeah." I patted Blizz as she trotted in to say hi. "You missed all the excitement."

Cody hovered in the doorway, looking distracted. "I heard."

"So what's going on with Josie?" Frank asked.

He sounded a little too interested. Guess my little talk with him hadn't stuck. Oh well. Frank can be stubborn when he's sure he's right about something.

"I'm not sure." Cody ran a hand through his hair, leaving it standing up. "She's still in the office with my mom. Um, but listen, I'll catch you later, okay? I'm supposed to be, you know . . ."

He took off without another word, surprising even Blizz. The dog took off too, catching up to her master just before he disappeared around the corner at the end of the hall.

"What's with him?" I wondered.

Chet shrugged. "He's probably just upset that some random maid almost ruined his family's business." He wandered back into the playroom and grabbed my paddle, which I'd abandoned on the table. "I call next game."

We messed around in the playroom for another hour or so. When regular Ping-Pong got boring, we invented our own rules. We were on our fourth game of Sudden Death Torpedo Pong when my stomach grumbled.

"Hey, it's lunchtime," I said, checking my watch. "Let's get over there. Maybe if that wildlife lecture is still going on, we'll beat the rush."

Frank rolled his eyes. "Yeah, some rush," he said. "Us and, like, a dozen other people. Call out the crowd control specialists."

Chet chuckled. "I'm with Joe. Let's eat!"

We tossed our paddles back on the shelf and headed for the door. As we reached the hall, there was a sudden loud shriek from somewhere nearby.

"Who was that?" Chet exclaimed.

I was already running. "Let's find out."

The three of us rounded the corner into the staff hallway. Josie was standing there, staring into a doorway about halfway down the hall. Toy Toy was wiggling in her arms and barking.

"Josie?" Frank said as we hurried over. "What's wrong?"

"My room!" she cried, pointing through the open door.

I'd reached her by then and turned to look. "Whoa!" I said. "Looks like it's been ransacked!"

LIES 11

FRANK

STARED INTO THE BEDROOM, ONLY VAGUELY aware that Joe was questioning Josie. The place was totally trashed. Dresser drawers had been pulled out and upended, strewing clothes everywhere. The desk lamp was tipped over. Books were lying on the floor near the bookcase. The bedspread was wadded up in the middle of the floor. Even Toy Toy's food dishes and box of puppy pads had been tossed around. If Josie was behind all the mischief at the lodge, why would she ransack her own room?

"I just found it like this," Josie was saying in response to Joe's questions. She sounded upset. No wonder. "I've been with Mrs. G until just now. It looked normal when I left for breakfast."

"So you've been with Mrs. Gallagher since we saw you last?" I asked.

Josie nodded, looking pale. "I just got here. I wanted to get Toy Toy a snack before lunch."

"But who would do something like this to your room?" Chet sounded confused. "I thought you were the only one causing trouble around here."

"Exactly what I was thinking." I stared at Josie. "Want to retract that confession?"

"What?" Josie blinked at me. "No! I don't know who did this. But I did all that other stuff, like I said. I swear."

"Okay," Joe said. "So where's Poppy's music player? And that kid's boots?"

Josie's expression wavered. "I'm—not sure yet. Like I said, I probably moved them around by mistake." She darted into the room and grabbed a box of dog treats out of the mess. "I'd better go tell someone about this," she said, hurrying off down the hall.

Joe, Chet, and I followed more slowly. "Well?" Joe said. "Do we believe her?"

"No," I said, at the same time Chet said, "Maybe."

We reached the lobby and had to stop talking about it for a while, since Stanley was there complaining to Poppy about how boring the wildlife lecture had been. Typical.

But as soon as we got our food, the three of us settled at a table in the corner of the dining room.

"Okay," Joe said, digging into his lasagna. "So maybe you

were right, bro. Josie sure seems like she could be hiding something."

"Music to my ears." I smiled weakly. "Seriously, though, I'm sure of it now. Josie can't be the culprit."

"Just because she couldn't have messed up her own room, it doesn't mean she didn't do the stuff she confessed to." Chet's eyes lit up as he reached for the salt. "I know! What if one of her victims was getting revenge by ransacking her room?"

"You mean like me? I almost wiped out on the stairs, remember?" Joe grinned and crossed his heart. "But I didn't wreck Josie's room—I swear!"

"Actually, I was thinking of Stanley." Chet shrugged. "He seems pretty upset about everything that's happened. What if he thinks Josie was really trying to kill him?"

"He does seem like the type to hold a grudge," Joe said.

"I suppose it's possible," I admitted. "Except Stanley was at that wildlife lecture, wasn't he? We just heard him talking about it. There's his alibi."

"Sure. But we don't know when that ended." Joe glanced around the room. "Hang on a sec. . . ."

He hurried off. I stirred my soup, still thinking about Chet's theory. Stanley definitely seemed eager to spread blame around whenever possible. But was he really the type of guy to trash someone's room in revenge?

Joe returned after a moment. "Well?" Chet asked.

"Inconclusive." Joe shook his head. "Apparently the

lecture let out about twenty minutes ago. But it lasted a long time, so just about everyone left to use the bathroom at least once."

"Including Stanley?" I asked.

Joe nodded. "Including Stanley. At least that's what Nate said."

We continued discussing the situation while we ate. But we didn't reach any real conclusions. At least Joe and Chet now agreed that Josie might have been lying in her confession. But how could we prove it one way or the other?

"The key to all this seems to be Stanley," I said as I wadded up my napkin and tossed it on my empty plate. "I think we need to find out a little more about the guy."

"You mean talk to him?" Joe looked less than thrilled by the idea.

"No," I said. "I was thinking we could tail him for a while. See where he goes, what he does. Whom he annoys."

"Oh." Joe looked much more interested. "Okay, cool."

"What about Josie?" Chet asked. "Shouldn't we follow her, too?"

I shrugged. "I don't think we have to worry about her. After her confession, I doubt the Gallaghers will let her out of their sight for long. That gives me an idea, though—why don't you talk to a few people, see if anyone has any opinions about Josie? Feel out whether she really might have done what she claims she did."

Chet agreed. He headed off to talk to the honeymooners,

who were eating over near the window. Stanley wasn't in the dining room, so Joe and I headed into the lobby.

"There," Joe said in a low voice.

Stanley was sitting near the fire, flipping through a magazine. He didn't look up as Joe and I strolled past, settling in another seating area behind him.

He also didn't notice when we followed him as he finally headed in to eat lunch. Or when we stayed just out of sight while he wandered down the hallway, picking his nose. Or when we waited outside the men's room until he emerged, still buckling his belt. Or listened from a discreet distance as he complained to Mrs. Gallagher about the texture of his bath towels.

Yeah. I'd been on more interesting stakeouts, that was for sure.

Basically, for the next two hours we followed Stanley as he wandered aimlessly around the lodge. Joe started to look fed up after a while.

"Is this guy ever going to do anything interesting?" he whispered as we tailed him down the hallway leading to the hot tub lounge.

I didn't answer. Stanley had stopped short halfway to the lounge. "Shh," I hushed Joe, pulling him into an alcove.

Then I peeked out—just in time to see Stanley glance in both directions before ducking out of sight through a door. Luckily, he didn't seem to see me.

"Where'd he go?" Joe whispered, looking out.

"Not sure." I led the way to the door. The sign on it read KITCHEN: STAFF ONLY.

"Weird," Joe said. "Let's take a look."

"Careful," I warned.

Joe pushed the door open a crack, then quickly let it fall shut. "He's in there," he confirmed quietly. "Looks like he's the only one in there right now, actually. If we open the door, he'll see us for sure. Should we go in? Maybe tell him we're looking for a snack or something?"

"No, stay here," I said. "I'll run to the dining room in case he comes out that way."

The dining room was deserted except for the other maid/waitress, a woman in her thirties whose name I couldn't remember. Since the blizzard had started, it wasn't only the rules about dogs being out around the guests that had been relaxed. Most of the staff wasn't bothering to wear uniforms or name tags anymore either.

"Hello, sir," the woman greeted me pleasantly. "Can I help you?"

I thought fast. "Um, is there any coffee left?"

She waved a hand at the coffee station. "Sure, help yourself."

As she went back to work wiping down the tables, I busied myself pouring and stirring a cup, keeping one eye on the door to the kitchen. But there was no sign of Stanley.

A moment later I heard a short whistle. Glancing over, I saw Joe gesturing from the side doorway. Leaving the coffee behind, I hurried over.

"He just came out," Joe said quietly. "Heading back to the lobby, I think."

"Did he have food with him?" I asked.

Joe shrugged. "Not that I saw. If he was getting a snack, he must have eaten it in there."

I nodded and followed Joe toward the lobby. Was Stanley's detour into the deserted kitchen suspicious? Or was he just helping himself to a between-meals bite? I had no idea.

By the time we reached the lobby, Stanley was nowhere in sight. But Chet spotted us and rushed over. He looked kind of excited.

"There you guys are!" he exclaimed. "Can we talk?"

"Sure. Did you find out anything?" I asked.

Chet glanced around. Unlike the kitchen and dining room, the lobby was fairly busy. The Richmond kids were tossing a ball around in the corner. Mr. Gallagher was chatting with the honeymooners, who were settled in near the fire, looking cozy. Mrs. Gallagher and the lodge's chef were huddled over some paperwork on one of the big wooden coffee tables. Mr. and Mrs. Richmond were over by the windows, sipping drinks and gazing out at the swirling snow.

None of them were paying any attention to us, but Chet gestured for Joe and me to follow him into an unoccupied corner behind the racks of brochures advertising local restaurants and other attractions.

"Okay, so I was talking to the chef," he began in a low voice.

"In the kitchen?" I shot Joe a look, wondering if this was connected somehow to Stanley's recent pit stop.

Chet shook his head. "I ran into her in the hall near her room. I started asking about all the staff—you know, so she wouldn't get suspicious of me wanting to know about Josie."

"Why would she get suspicious, dude?" Joe asked with a grin. "Everyone in the lodge knows about Josie's confession."

"Whatever." Chet frowned slightly. "The point is, she told me something interesting about Rick."

"Rick Ferguson? What about him?" I asked, keeping an eye on the doorways in case Stanley came in.

"Apparently Rick has a criminal past!" Chet said.

That got my full attention. "What do you mean, a criminal past?"

"He's a felon," Chet said. "The chef didn't know all the details, but she was sure of that part. I guess the Gallaghers gave him a chance to turn his life around when they opened this place, like, fifteen years ago. And Rick's been here ever since."

"I guess that's interesting," Joe said. "Not exactly surprising, though. Rick looks like a guy who's done some living, if you know what I mean."

I nodded, but I was distracted by the sound of a raised voice. It was Nate. He'd just stood up from his spot near the fireplace, looking annoyed.

"Well, I hope it turns up soon," he exclaimed, his voice

carrying as he glared at Mr. Gallagher. "I'd just come to the exciting part!"

"What's going on over there?" Joe followed my gaze.

"Not sure. Let's find out." I stepped closer.

"I'm sorry, Nate," Mr. Gallagher was saying soothingly. "I'm sure your book will turn up. Maybe one of the other guests borrowed it without realizing it was yours."

"You lost your book?" I asked.

Nate glanced at me and frowned. "I didn't lose it. I left it on the table over there while Cassie and I were taking a walk. When I came back to get it just now, it was gone!"

He sounded a lot like that little kid with the missing boots. Was this the same sort of situation? Was Nate so distracted by his beautiful new bride that he couldn't keep track of where he'd left things? Or had the book really disappeared?

"If someone found it, they might have returned it to the library," Mr. Gallagher suggested. "Let's go take a look, shall we?"

"It's not that big of a deal," Cassie spoke up, scurrying after Nate and Mr. Gallagher as they headed off across the lobby. "I'm sure it will turn up."

"So something else has disappeared," I said.

Joe shrugged. "Yeah, a book. Why would someone bother to steal something like that? It's not like they can sell it on the black market for big bucks."

"Can't do that with a pair of little kid boots, either," I

pointed out. "I'm thinking either the disappearances are a coincidence, or someone's just out to cause mischief."

"Why?" Joe wondered.

Chet looked worried. "Maybe someone's trying to ruin the Gallaghers," he said. "If things keep going wrong, I'm sure people will talk about it, and—"

He was cut off by a sudden loud hum that seemed to come from every direction at once.

A second later all the lights went off!

DARKER 12

JOE

H EY!" SOMEONE YELLED. IT SOUNDED like Frank, but I couldn't be sure. With the lights off, it was pretty dark in the lobby despite the huge windows. The heavy snow still falling outside blocked most of the light. Only the eerie orange glow of the fireplace offered any real illumination.

"Calm down, everyone!" Mr. Gallagher's voice rang out over a chorus of shouts and murmurs of alarm, along with the wails of at least a few of the Richmond children. "We'll get this sorted out. In the meantime, everyone please stay where you are."

The chaos soon subsided, at least somewhat. Mr. Gallagher hurried off to check on whether the rest of the lodge had power. Meanwhile Mrs. Gallagher and the chef started digging up candles and flashlights and distributing them to everyone. When she reached us, Mrs. Gallagher handed me a fat candle in an old-fashioned cast-iron holder.

"Can you be trusted with fire, Joe?" she asked with a wink.

I grinned. "Sure thing, Mrs. G. I've only burned down a few minor landmarks."

She snorted and moved on. "Careful with that," Frank said as I lit the candle.

I rolled my eyes. "Thanks, Mom." The candle sputtered and took, casting a tiny circle of cheerful yellow light. I held it up near my chin and made a monster face at Chet, who snickered. This was actually kind of fun—like camping.

Well, it would be fun if there wasn't a possible attempted murderer around, anyway. . . .

I forgot about that as the second maid came into the lobby, followed by Poppy, who was wielding a small flashlight. "So it's not just my room that went dark," Poppy said to the room at large. "What happened?"

"Some kind of temporary outage," Mrs. Gallagher told her. "We'll have it sorted out soon."

"Oh." Poppy looked mildly dismayed. "I'm glad I was just reading a book and not in the shower or something."

As she wandered off to talk to the honeymooners, Mr. Gallagher returned. Rick was with him.

"Seems to be a general outage," the lodge owner announced. "The generator must have cut off."

"Why?" Mr. Richmond sounded nervous. "Does this mean we won't have any heat?"

"Please try not to worry," Mrs. Gallagher said. "My husband and Rick will go out right now and get it running again."

"I'll come too," Chet volunteered, stepping forward. "I'm pretty good at tinkering around with mechanical stuff."

"Yeah," I muttered to Frank with a grin. "As long as the stuff in question isn't the engine of a certain creaky old jalopy."

But Mr. Gallagher was nodding gratefully at Chet. "We can use an extra set of hands," he said. "Come on." He glanced at his wife. "Send Cody out to help us if you see him."

"Should we go too?" Frank asked. "We're both pretty handy."

I shrugged, not really in the mood to plunge out into the storm. "Let them handle it," I said. "Chet will come get us if he thinks we can be useful."

Glancing around the room, I realized that almost everyone was gathered in one room. It reminded me of those old-school mysteries where the detective gathers everyone together and announces the identity of the murderer. Too bad Frank and I hadn't solved our mystery.

"Where's Stanley?" Frank broke into my thoughts. "I'm surprised he hasn't turned up to complain about this yet."

I realized he was right. "Who knows? With his luck, he probably was in the shower when it happened."

As if on cue, Stanley burst into the lobby. "What's going on?" he exclaimed loudly. His hair looked damp in the dim, flickering light, and I grinned and elbowed Frank.

"Looks like I called it, dude," I whispered as Stanley bustled over to complain to Mrs. Gallagher.

A few minutes later Chet walked in, breathless and pink-cheeked and shaking off the snow. He stopped in the middle of the room.

"They sent me in to say the power will be back on in a few minutes," he announced loudly to murmurs of relief and one irritated-sounding "About time!" from Stanley.

Then Chet hurried over. "They kick you out when they heard about the Queen?" I joked.

Chet didn't seem to hear me. He glanced around to make sure nobody was close enough to eavesdrop.

"This is bad," he whispered, running a hand through his snow-dampened hair. "The generator going out was no accident. The wires were cut!"

"What?" Frank and I said in one voice.

Chet nodded grimly. "No question about it. Somebody did it on purpose."

"But why?" I almost immediately realized the answer to my own question. "Unless it's to make this place look bad."

"Again," Frank added with a nod. "Are they really going to be able to get it up and running again?"

"Yeah, sounds like it," Chet replied. "That Rick guy is really handy. Cody, too—he and Blizz turned up a minute ago."

"I wonder . . . ," Frank began.

I elbowed him when I saw Poppy heading our way. "Never a dull moment around here, huh?" she said cheerfully.

"Right." I decided it couldn't hurt to do a little investigating while we waited for the power to come on. "Um, so you were upstairs in your room when it happened, huh?"

She nodded. "What were you guys doing? Have you gone to any of the extra activities today?"

"No, we've pretty much been entertaining ourselves," Frank said.

Out of the corner of my eye, I saw the chef hand Stanley a plate with several cookies on it. "Excuse me a sec."

Leaving Poppy talking to Frank and Chet, I hurried over to intercept the chef as she left Stanley with his food. She'd been willing to talk to Chet earlier. Maybe I could get the answer to a question I'd been wondering about.

"Can I ask you something?" I said. "How do you all put up with that guy?" I gestured at Stanley, who had his back to us as he wolfed down his cookies.

"Who, Mr. Wright?" The chef glanced at him, then shrugged. "Just part of the job."

"Okay," I said. "But the guy is seriously obnoxious. It's not like anyone would blame you if you didn't wait on him hand and foot, you know?"

The chef hesitated, glancing in Stanley's direction again. Then she winked. "Okay, I admit it. The cash helps."

"Cash?" I echoed.

She nodded. "Mr. Wright likes to play the big spender," she whispered. "He's been waving cash around at all of us since he arrived." She shot me a slightly suspicious look. "Why do you ask?"

"No reason. Just curious." I gave her my most winning smile, then wandered off. So Stanley had been flashing money at the staff to get better service. That explained a lot—like why Josie had been so worried about him after his near miss out in the storm.

Wanting to confirm that, I glanced around. But Josie was nowhere in sight. And I didn't quite dare go up to Mrs. Gallagher and ask if that was why they were being so nice to Stanley—because he was bringing a lot of extra cash into their struggling business.

Did it mean anything? I wasn't sure. But I went over to fill in Frank and Chet just in case.

. . .

By bedtime the storm was still going strong, though power had been back on for long enough that most of the guests seemed to have forgotten about the outage. Frank, Chet, and I were definitely not among those guests, however.

"There must be a way to figure out who could have sneaked outside long enough to cut those generator wires," I said as I watched Frank kick off his slippers and flop onto his bed.

He yawned. "At least we can rule out a few people," he said. "Starting with everyone who was in the lobby with us when the lights cut off."

"And Poppy, who was up in her room," I added.

To be honest, I was feeling frustrated by our lack of progress on the case. How hard could it be to pick a trouble-maker out of a couple of dozen people? There had to be clues we were missing.

I crawled into bed and turned off the light. Could Frank and I be off our game? I was really starting to wonder. . . .

The next morning I woke up early, not feeling particularly well rested. It had taken longer than usual to fall asleep. And my dreams had been restless, filled with barking dogs and shouting, though I couldn't remember many details.

The snow was still coming down outside, but it had definitely slowed. The wind had died down too.

"Looks like the storm's almost over," Chet said hopefully.

I yawned. "About time. Let's get downstairs—I'm in serious need of coffee."

But when we entered the dining room, we got a caffeine-free wakeup call that jolted me to full attention. The place was a mess!

Well, not the entire place. But several tables were over-turned near the kitchen door, and food wrappers and shred-ded napkins were scattered here and there.

"What happened?" I called to Cody, who was rushing past with a bucket in his hand and Blizz at his heels.

He stopped and looked at us, his face weary. "Raccoons," he said grimly. "Somehow a window in the kitchen got broken, and they came in last night. Took a while to chase them all out. Luckily, Blizz smelled them before they had a chance to get any farther into the lodge. Woke me up by barking and scratching at the door."

I nodded, my weird dog dreams suddenly making a lot more sense. "Good girl," I said, giving Blizz a pat.

"Cody!" Mr. Gallagher shouted from across the room. "A little help over here?"

Cody hurried off. "Raccoons?" Frank said. "I thought they hibernated in the winter."

The honeymooners walked into the room just in time to hear him. "Actually, they don't," Nate said. "We learned all about it at the wildlife lecture yesterday. They're less active at this time of year, but they're not true hibernators, and . . ."

His voice trailed off as he got a look around. "What happened here?"

By the time we finished explaining what Cody had just told us, the staff had most of the tables back in place. As Rick swept up the rest of the trash, Mrs. Gallagher clapped her hands.

"Attention, guests," she called out. "Sorry for the disruption. We'll have it cleaned up soon, but in the meantime, please enjoy your breakfast." She gestured at the buffet table, where Josie and the other waitress were busy setting out food.

"Excellent," Chet said, patting his belly. "Let's go."

We headed over, ending up at the head of the line. "How do you think that window got broken?" I asked Frank in a low voice as Chet grabbed a plate and moved forward.

Frank shrugged. "Maybe our culprit," he replied quietly. "Maybe the storm. Or the raccoons. We should try to get a look at it if we can."

I nodded, reaching for a plate. Chet was already helping himself to a large stack of waffles.

"Hey, is that a chocolate chip one back there?" he asked eagerly, grabbing a waffle sitting on a plate behind the others.

"Wait!" Josie exclaimed. "That's Mr. Wright's special order. He'll freak out if someone else eats it!"

"Too late," I said with a grin.

Chet's eyes widened with alarm as he bit down on the waffle. For a second I thought he felt guilty because of what Josie had said.

Then I gasped as he spit the half-chewed waffle into his hand—along with a mouthful of blood!

OUT FOR BLOOD

13

FRANK

I HEARD JOE'S GASP AND TURNED TO SEE blood dripping out of Chet's mouth. "Ow!" he mumbled.

"Chet! What happened?" I cried, leaping toward him.

By now others had noticed the blood as well. There were screams and cries of alarm. Mrs. Gallagher rushed over and started fussing over Chet, ordering him to open his mouth so she could see inside.

"Stand back, please!" the older waitress said, gesturing to the other guests, who were gathering around looking shocked and worried. "Give them some room."

The waffle had fallen to the floor. I grabbed it just before it got trampled by Joe, who was leaping around, telling Chet to hold still.

I punched him lightly in the shoulder to get his attention.

"Check it out," I said grimly, holding up the waffle. Several shards of glass were poking out of the ragged edge where Chet had bitten!

Joe let out a low whistle. "That's hardcore," he said with a worried glance at Chet.

I tapped Mrs. Gallagher on the arm. "Look," I said. "There was glass in the waffle."

Chet still had his mouth wide open, but his eyes widened with alarm. "Did you swallow any, dude?" Joe asked him.

Chet shook his head and closed his mouth. "I don't think so," he said, his words slightly garbled. "I stopped chewing when Josie yelled."

"Good thing she yelled when she did, then." I shot a look at Josie, who was clutching the edge of the buffet table and staring at Chet in horror. "Someone could die from a stunt like this."

"Like Chet." Joe stared at our friend with concern.

I nodded. "Or Stanley," I reminded him quietly, trying not to let anyone else hear. "That waffle was meant for him."

"Come with me, Chet," Mrs. Gallagher said briskly. "You've got a couple of pretty nasty cuts on your tongue and the roof of your mouth. I want to check you out in the infirmary."

She led him away. "Is he going to be okay?" Josie cried, her voice high and sort of fluttery.

"Looks like it," I told her. "Where'd that waffle come from?"

Josie didn't seem to hear me. Her eyes were wide and anxious as she stared after Chet. "This is terrible," she moaned. "Just terrible!"

"I know," I said. "I—"

I cut myself off as Josie burst into tears and raced away, crashing out through the side door. "Stay here," I told Joe quickly. "Talk to anyone you can."

Joe nodded. "On it, bro."

I took off after Josie. By the time I burst into the hall outside the dining room, she was nowhere in sight. I jogged to the lobby. She wasn't there, either, though the Richmonds were comforting their crying kids. I hoped they weren't too traumatized by Chet's bloody mouth, but I couldn't worry about that right now. Skirting around them, I hurried down the hall leading to the staff's quarters.

Someone was over by the side doors, but it wasn't Josie. It was Stanley. Realizing I hadn't seen him yet that morning, I paused. He was holding his parka, shaking it vigorously and sending drops of water flying everywhere. Nice. Making another big mess for someone else to clean up.

He noticed me looking. "What do you want?" he snarled.

"Nothing." I rolled my eyes and continued around the corner into the staff hallway.

I reached Josie's room. The door was slightly ajar, so I gave it a light push. The room was empty.

Okay, where could she have gone? While I stood there thinking, I heard a faint yap. Toy Toy!

Following the sound, I realized it was coming from the back stairwell. I peered in through the glass part of the door.

Josie was in there, but she wasn't alone. She was facing off against Cody. Toy Toy was leaping around the humans' feet and letting out an occasional yip.

I could see both Josie and Cody's faces in profile. Josie was still crying, and Cody looked angry and appeared to be talking fast. Was he questioning her about what had just happened? I bit my lip, wishing I could hear what they were saying. But if I opened the door, they'd know I was there.

The sound of footsteps distracted me. Turning, I saw Rick hurrying down the hall. His eyes were down, and he didn't notice me standing there in the stairwell alcove as he rushed past.

With one more glance at Josie, I turned to follow Rick. He was one of our suspects too—and a felon. He'd been in the dining room during the waffle incident. And now here he was, racing along, looking tense.

Staying out of sight, I hurried along behind him as he rounded the corner and then ducked into a closet, emerging a moment later holding a hammer and a box of nails. I hid behind a potted plant until he rushed past again.

I tailed him to the kitchen. Mr. Gallagher was already there, holding a piece of plywood. The door to the side hall was propped open, and Rick hurried in.

"Let's do this," he said gruffly. "It's cold in here."

"Yeah," Mr. Gallagher agreed. "You find the nails?"

They were fixing the window. Okay, nothing suspicious about that. I almost left them to it, but Mr. Gallagher's next words stopped me.

"Don't tell my wife, but I don't think the wind broke this window," he said grimly.

Rick let out a snort of agreement. "No way," he said. "It broke from the inside out. Hard for the wind to do that."

I pressed my back against the wall, listening closely. They were silent for a moment, then Mr. Gallagher spoke again. "Let's not mention this to anyone," he said. "Because Stanley Wright is already threatening to sue, and if he finds out about more trouble . . ."

My eyes widened as his voice trailed off. Stanley was threatening to sue the lodge? That wasn't good. Especially if he found out about that waffle . . .

The men had gone quiet again, so I slipped away and went to look for Joe. He was in the lobby, watching the Richmond kids run around. They seemed to have recovered from their shock at Chet's accident, at least judging by the way they were shrieking and laughing as they chased one another.

"Find out anything?" I asked Joe.

"A little. The chef said Stanley provided his own waffle mix—gave it to her yesterday after complaining about the taste of her waffles."

"Typical." I snorted. "Think she got mad enough to slip some glass in there?"

"Maybe, but I doubt it. She seemed really upset." Joe shrugged. "Although she did admit to making his waffle batter first and leaving it sitting around in the kitchen while she made the rest." He smiled grimly. "That means just about anyone could've slipped in long enough to tamper with it. Or they could've messed with the mix last night." He sighed. "So, not too useful, I guess. Did you catch Josie?"

"Not exactly . . ." I glanced around to make sure nobody was close enough to hear me. The Richmond parents and Poppy were there, but all of them were over near the fireplace.

So I told Joe what I'd overheard in the kitchen. "Wow," Joe said. "Why am I not surprised that Stanley would try to sue?"

"I know, right?" I said. "I guess that's all the more reason someone might want to shut him up."

Just then Mrs. Gallagher arrived. Joe and I rushed over.

"How's Chet?" Joe demanded. "Where is he?"

"He's resting in the infirmary with an ice pack on his face," Mrs. Gallagher reported. "I gave him something for the pain, and something to help him sleep a little."

"Wow, he must be hurting if he actually needs help to sleep," Joe joked weakly.

Mrs. Gallagher smiled. "Don't worry, boys. Chet should be just fine, though his mouth will be sore for a while. Luckily the cuts aren't deep, and I only had to pick one shard out of his tongue."

I winced at the thought of that. Poor Chet!

A couple of the Richmond kids raced over. "We're bored!" the little girl announced. "Do you have any more toys?"

"There might be a few things in one of the cabinets," Mrs. Gallagher told the kids, gesturing at the shelving system built into one of the walls. "Why don't you take a look?"

"Yay!" the little boy yelled. He raced over to the cabinets and started flinging open all the doors he could reach.

"Not the ones on the bottom row," Mrs. Gallagher called. "Try a little farther up."

But the boy was staring into one of the cabinets, a small one built into the narrow area at the edge of the fireplace. "Hey!" he shouted. "My boots!"

Joe and I wandered over just as the kid pulled out a pair of red snow boots. "Are those the boots that got lost?" I said in surprise.

"Not lost." The little boy glared at me. "Stolen!"

"How did those get in there?" Mrs. Gallagher bent to peer into the cabinet. "Oh, my!"

She pulled out several other items—a pair of sunglasses, a baseball cap, a paperback book, and an MP3 player.

"It's all the missing stuff!" Joe exclaimed. "How'd it get in there?"

"I have no idea." Mrs. Gallagher looked confused. "We don't store much stuff in the lowest row of cabinets."

"What's this?" Joe bent and poked at another item in the

pile, a raggedy bit of cloth in the shape of a bone. "Looks like a dog toy."

"That must belong to Toy Toy." Mrs. Gallagher sounded distracted as she gathered up the other items. "I'd better start returning these things to their rightful owners."

As she hurried off, Joe and I stared at each other. "Weird," he said. "Think Josie did it?"

"Why would she steal her own dog's toy?" I nudged the cloth bone with my toe.

Joe shrugged and grabbed the toy. "Let's go ask her."

I couldn't think of a better idea, so I followed. Josie wasn't in the dining room or kitchen or any of the other public spaces in the lodge. Come to think of it, I hadn't seen her since witnessing her argument with Cody earlier. I filled Joe in on that incident, which left us both wondering: where had she gone?

"Better check her room," Joe said, leading the way to the staff's quarters.

We knocked on Josie's door, which was closed now, but there was no answer. "Josie?" I called. "You in there?"

"What are you guys doing?" It was Cody. He'd just rounded the corner at the end of the hall.

"Looking for Josie." Realizing he might be the last person who'd seen her, I added, "Have any idea where she might be?"

"No, why would I?" he replied quickly. Then he shrugged. "Hang on. I was just coming to get Blizz. She had a busy night with those raccoons, so I stuck her in my room to nap after breakfast."

He hurried over to his door and pushed it open. All three of us gasped as frigid air blew out at us.

"Hey!" Cody shouted, rushing in.

Joe and I followed. The room's two windows were wide open, and snow was pouring in!

HOT AND COLD

14

JOE

BLIZZ BARKED AS FRANK AND I ENTERED the freezing-cold room. With her thick fur coat, she was in a lot better shape than we were. I was already shivering as I helped Frank wrestle one of the windows shut. Cody was working on the other, kicking snow out of the way with his sneakers.

Soon both windows were closed and locked. "What a mess!" I exclaimed, brushing snow off my shirt. "How'd it happen?"

Blizz seemed bright-eyed and happy as she sniffed at the snowy floor. Cody watched her, frowning slightly. "I don't know," he said. "I'd better grab a mop to clean this up."

We followed him out of the room. Blizz came along, her tail wagging.

"Good thing it was Blizz in there and not Toy Toy," I joked, giving the dog a pat. "Poor little Toy Toy isn't used to facing the cold without his full winter wardrobe."

Frank chuckled, but his eyes looked serious. "Seems like our saboteur might've struck again," he said as soon as Cody was out of earshot.

"Yeah." I shrugged. "So let's get back to work."

We decided to start by checking out the scenes of the various crimes. There was nothing much to see in the stairwell or by the side exit, and Josie still wasn't answering her door. We couldn't very well go look at the ski trail at the moment—the snow was lighter than ever, but the wind had picked up again, blowing the drifts around—so we headed for the kitchen next.

The chef was puttering around near the stove when we came in. "What can I do for you, boys?" she asked.

"Nothing," Frank said. "Um, Mr. G just asked us to check on the window. See if it's letting any cold air in."

That seemed to satisfy the woman. She returned to whatever she was doing, humming tunelessly under her breath. Frank and I headed for the boarded-up window. Nothing seemed out of place inside, so I opened the next window and stuck my head out into the cold.

"See anything?" Frank asked.

"Hard to see much with the snow blowing in my face," I complained. "Wait—what's that?"

The wind had just shifted the snow banked up against

the building, revealing a flash of silver. Another gust covered it so quickly I would have missed it if I'd blinked.

I pulled my head inside. "There's something in the snow out there," I told Frank. "Give me a boost."

Frank looked dubious, but offered me a leg up. "Don't get frostbite," he joked.

"Trust me, I'm not planning to stay out there long." I hoisted myself over the window frame. "Just make sure nobody locks up behind me. Or if they do, call Blizz!"

"Hey!" the chef said, finally noticing what was going on. "What are you two doing?"

Then I dropped to the ground and couldn't hear her clearly anymore. Brr! It was cold out there. Really cold. Wrapping my arms around myself, I stepped carefully toward the base of the other window.

Okay, a real detective would probably slow down at this point, be careful not to disturb the scene too much. But I was too cold to take things slowly. Instead I kicked at the drifted snow until I felt my foot hit something hard.

"Aha!" I muttered through lips that were already half-frozen.

Bending down, I dug into the snow. My hands started to go numb almost immediately, but it was easy to feel what I was looking for. Mostly because whatever it was poked me in the finger.

"Ouch," I yelped, yanking my hand back.

Then I reached down into the snow more carefully. This

time I pulled out the object—a large pair of stainless-steel scissors.

"You okay out there?" Frank was looking out the window.

"Yeah. Got it." I hurried over, tucking the scissors into my back pocket so he could pull me up with both hands.

Inside the warm kitchen, I showed Frank what I'd found. "Scissors?" he said.

The chef gasped and hurried over. "My kitchen shears!" she cried, grabbing the scissors. "I've been looking for those all day!"

"How'd they get outside?" I wondered.

She shrugged, cradling the scissors like a baby. "Search me. Last I saw them was yesterday after I washed them and left them in the rack to dry."

She hurried off toward the sink, and my brother and I traded a look. "Scissors," Frank said again, more quietly this time so the chef couldn't hear. "Think those things would cut a generator wire?"

"They're pretty sharp." I sucked a drop of blood off my finger where the scissors had poked me. "Still doesn't tell us who did it."

"Yeah." Frank glanced at the chef as she disappeared through the door to the dining room. "The kitchen's never locked, as far as I know. Anyone could've wandered in and grabbed those scissors anytime the chef's back was turned."

I nodded. "Maybe the same person who messed with that waffle."

At that moment Mr. Gallagher burst into the kitchen. "Oh, hello, boys," he said, sounding almost cheerful. "I was looking for Chef, but I might as well tell you, too. I just called the county for the weather update, and it's good news for once."

"Really?" I said, wiggling my toes inside my sneakers. They were still half-frozen.

"The worst of the storm has passed," the lodge owner said. "The roads should be passable again by tomorrow morning."

"Great." Frank smiled weakly. I could guess what he was thinking. That didn't leave us much time to solve the case!

We hurried out into the hallway. "We need to talk to Josie," I said. "Where could she be?"

Frank looked troubled. "Do you really think she put glass in that waffle?" he asked. "It doesn't make sense. She already confessed—why pull another stunt? Especially a potentially deadly one like that?"

I shrugged. "Who knows? She seems pretty emotional. Maybe she wasn't thinking straight."

"Maybe." Frank didn't sound convinced. "I guess we should talk to her either way. It's not like we've got any other hot leads."

We resumed our search. We didn't find Josie, but we

spotted Cody and Blizz walking down the side hall. "Cody! Hold up!" I called, jogging to catch up to him. "Have you seen Josie?"

"Didn't you already ask me that?" he said with a crooked half smile.

Frank shrugged. "We still haven't found her. We're starting to get worried."

"Yeah," I agreed. "The girl's a little unhinged. Who knows what she could be up to?"

Cody frowned. "She's not crazy," he said sharply. "Just maybe a little emotional, and, um . . ."

He was starting to look a little emotional himself. "Dude," I said, peering into his face. "What's wrong? Are you afraid she'll come after you next?"

"Maybe she already did," Frank pointed out. "Those windows in his room didn't open themselves. And I seriously doubt Blizz did it."

I gasped as I realized something. "No, Blizz didn't open the windows!" I exclaimed. "But she didn't stop someone else from doing it either."

Frank glanced at me. "What do you mean?"

"Blizz wouldn't let some random person come into her room and mess around, right?" I asked Cody. "She'd only let someone she trusted in. Like you, or your folks, or maybe—"

"Josie," Frank finished. "Good catch, bro!"

"Thanks." I was still watching Cody. His face sort of crumpled. "Cody? What's wrong?"

Cody glanced down the hall as the honeymooners wandered into view. "Can we go somewhere private to talk?" he said. "Chet's told me a few things about you guys, and with all your questions . . . well, there's something you probably need to know."

Okay, so it sounded like he was on to us. But what did he need to tell us? Did he know more about Josie than he'd let on so far? Or was there someone else he wanted to talk about—maybe Rick, or the chef, or someone we hadn't even thought of yet?

"Sure, let's go talk," Frank said.

"Let's not make it your room, though, Cody," I added. "I'm still warming up from playing in the snow." At his confused look, I shook my head. "Never mind. Let's go to the infirmary—we should check on Chet anyway. And if you've got something important to say, he will want to hear it."

Chet was sitting on a cot looking groggy when we walked in. Nobody else was in the infirmary, a tiny, sterile-white room tucked in behind the office.

"Hi," Chet mumbled, sounding as if he was talking through a mouthful of cotton. No wonder—the lower half of his face was swollen to twice its usual size. He tried to smile when Blizz walked over and licked his hand, though he was only semi-successful.

"How are you feeling?" Frank asked.

Chet just shrugged. "Been better." He eyed Cody. "What's with you, dude? You look kind of weird."

"I have a confession to make," Cody blurted out. "But you guys have to promise not to tell anyone."

Chet looked confused. Frank and I traded a look. "Just tell us, Cody," Frank said.

Cody took a deep breath. "Josie and I—we—um, we're sort of . . . a couple."

I stared at him. Whatever I'd been expecting him to say, that wasn't it. "A couple?" I said. "Like, a *couple* couple?"

"We've been together for about six months now," Cody said. "But we don't want my parents to find out—we don't think they'd approve."

"Why not?" Frank asked. "Josie seems . . . nice."

Yeah, nice and crazy, I thought. But I didn't say it out loud.

Cody shrugged. "They just wouldn't," he said. "Especially now. It's killing me to see her taking the fall for all the stuff that's been going on around here. Especially since I know she's just trying to protect me."

"Protect you?" Frank said sharply. "What do you mean? Why would she need to protect you?"

Cody sighed and rubbed his face, not quite meeting anyone's gaze. "Because I removed that closed sign from the ski slope the other day," he confessed.

I gasped. This guy was full of surprises!

"You did that?" I cried. "Why?"

Cody rubbed Blizz on the head. "I was trying to set up a little rescue scene," he admitted. "It seems stupid now, but it made sense at the time. I figured some beginner would go down the slope and get in trouble on the ice. Then Blizz and I could track him there, be the big heroes, maybe get some free publicity for the lodge. . . ." He shrugged. "People love any kind of news story with an animal in it, right?"

"Wow." I was having trouble taking this in. Cody had been right there when Frank had noticed the missing sign. If I hadn't jumped in, Stanley would have been his "rescue" story!

"The trouble is," Cody continued, "when I told Josie about my plan, she was totally freaked out—thought it was too dangerous. I tried to explain that the ice patch wasn't that bad, so it was seriously unlikely anyone could actually get injured, but she still acted like I was some kind of lunatic for wanting to try it." He bit his lip, shooting us a sidelong glance. "But I had to try something. Mom and Dad have actually started to talk about trying to sell the lodge if business doesn't pick up soon."

He sounded miserable. Chet's eyes were wide. "Dude!" he said.

"So what about the other stuff that's happened?" Frank sounded disapproving. "The locked door, the icy stairs, the generator, the glass in the waffle—were those more publicity stunts?"

"No!" Cody said immediately. "I'd never do anything like that. I didn't want anyone actually getting hurt." He looked miserable. "But try to tell Josie that! I keep telling her I don't know anything about those incidents, but she doesn't believe me. That's why she confessed—she's trying to protect me."

"So you didn't do any of the other bad stuff around here?" I asked.

"No. Well, except for messing up Josie's room—I did that." He shrugged. "I was trying to, you know—"

"Un-frame her for the crimes?" I suggested.

Cody nodded. "Pretty much."

"So you didn't do anything except remove that sign and trash Josie's room," Frank said. "And Josie didn't do anything at all—"

"Except open my windows earlier," Cody put in. "She was trying to make extra sure that nobody would suspect me of anything. Even though she thinks I'm a monster who's out to kill half our guests." He grimaced, somehow managing to look both annoyed and heartbroken at the same time.

"Wait," I said. "So when Frank saw you two arguing in the stairwell earlier . . ."

"You saw that?" Cody shot a surprised look at Frank, then shrugged. "Yeah, that was when she accused me of putting glass in the food. I can't believe she thinks I'd do something like that!"

I glanced at Frank and Chet. Frank looked thoughtful. Chet looked shocked and a little confused.

We spent a few more minutes questioning Cody. But I was pretty convinced that he was telling the truth, and I could tell Frank was too. Cody's confession also explained why Josie was so concerned about keeping the lodge in business. It wasn't just her job she was worried about—it was her boyfriend and his family.

Leaving Cody talking to Chet, we wandered out of the infirmary and down the hall. "Looks like we're back at square one," I said.

"Yeah. Guess we'd better look into some of the other suspects," Frank said. "Look—there's one of them now."

I followed his gaze. Rick was hurrying past at the end of the hall.

We took off after him, tailing him across the lobby and down the hall on the far side. When he disappeared outside through the side doors, Frank and I traded a look.

"You stay here—I'll go after him," I said. "I'm already soaked through from my last trip out into the snow. No sense both of us getting frostbite."

Not waiting for a response, I dove out into the waning storm. The wind was still whipping the drifts around, but the snow had almost stopped.

Rick was a dozen yards ahead, rounding the corner of the ski shack. If I wasn't mistaken, the generator shed was that way. Was he going out to check on it—or to tamper with it again?

I broke into a run, not wanting to lose sight of him. As

I rounded the corner, I spotted Rick just ahead. He paused and bent down to poke at something on the ground by his feet, muttering something that I couldn't make out due to the wind.

WHOOSH!

I gasped and jumped back as a huge pile of snow slid off the roof of the ski shack, completely burying Rick!

GUILTY 15

FRANK

I WAS LEANING AGAINST THE DOOR, THINKING about the case and wondering if it was time to give up, when I heard a shout from outside.

"Joe?" I murmured, shoving the door open.

"Frank!" Joe's voice came again, sounding frantic. "Help! Avalanche!"

Avalanche? That didn't make much sense, but I didn't hesitate. Diving out into the cold, I followed the sound of my brother's voice.

I rounded the corner to find Joe digging wildly in a huge pile of snow. "Rick's under here!" he cried. "We have to get him out!"

One look was enough to tell me we wouldn't have much chance by ourselves. "Keep digging," I said. "I'll get help."

I sprinted back into the lodge, shouting for help at the top of my lungs. Mr. Gallagher soon appeared, along with Nate, Cassie, and Poppy.

"It's Rick!" I cried. "He's buried in the snow out near the ski shack."

"What?" Mr. Gallagher's face went pale. He raced for the door.

Just then Cody appeared at the end of the hall. Blizz was at his side as usual. Suddenly remembering the dog's last rescue mission, I let out a whistle. Blizz bounded forward, followed by her master.

As soon as Cody heard what was happening, he took off for the door with Blizz at his heels. "She'll find him!" he called over his shoulder.

By the time I caught up, Blizz was trotting around the snow pile, her nose twitching as she searched. Joe, Mr. Gallagher, Cody, and Nate were there, too, flinging snow aside with their bare hands, but they were all watching the dog as they worked.

Finally Blizz let out a bark and started digging with her paws. "He's over here!" Cody shouted, dropping to his knees.

Soon we were all digging in that area. Joe let out a shout. "Found him!"

A hand flopped out of the snow. Mr. Gallagher grabbed it and pulled. "Rick!" he yelled. "Hang on, buddy!"

More hands reached to help, and seconds later we dragged Rick free. He was coughing and sputtering, his voice even hoarser than usual. "Careful," he wheezed out. "There's some kind of wire on the ground there, and . . ." Another bout of coughing overtook him.

"Never mind that, pal," Mr. Gallagher said. "You're going to be okay. Just breathe."

"We need to get him to the infirmary," Nate said. He grabbed the man's shoulders, while Mr. Gallagher and Cody each took a leg. Cassie was waiting to hold the door, so Joe and I just stayed out of the way until they rushed out of sight. Then we hurried inside ourselves.

"Oops," Joe said as a chunk of snow came off his shoe. "That's going to need a mop later."

"Never mind, it's not the first time someone . . ." I trailed off with a gasp. "That's it!"

"Huh?" Joe said.

My heart pounded as the puzzle pieces finally fell into place. "It was Stanley," I said. "I saw him right here earlier today. His jacket was wet, like he'd been out in the snow. Maybe he was out there setting up that 'avalanche'!"

Joe's eyes widened. "You're right! Right after we dug him out, Rick was muttering something about a wire."

At that moment, Stanley himself appeared at the bottom of the back stairs. "What's going on down here?" he complained. "I was trying to take a nap, and the shouting woke me up."

"Really?" Joe stared at him. "Is that true, or were you lurking around to see the results of your prank?"

Stanley frowned. "What are you talking about?"

"Give it up, Stanley. We know it was you." I stepped

closer. "I saw you coming in earlier. How'd you figure out how to rig that avalanche?"

"Yeah," Joe added. "And did you know it'd be Rick, or were you willing to take out whoever happened along?"

"I suppose you're the one who sabotaged the generator yesterday too," I said. "We should have guessed when we saw you wander in with wet hair after it happened."

Stanley's face darkened, and he glanced at the door. "You're crazy," he snapped. "You're probably the ones who messed up the generator. In fact, I'm going to go tell the Gallaghers that right now!"

He took off in the direction of the lobby. Joe and I followed.

When we arrived, board games were spread out on all the coffee tables. I vaguely remembered hearing something about a tournament happening that day—just another of the special snow-day activities. The Richmond kids were gathered around one game board, while their parents hovered nearby, staring in the direction of the infirmary with concern. The honeymooners were in the lobby too—Nate was warming himself in front of the fire while Cassie rubbed his back. Even Chet had emerged from his sickbed—probably because Rick needed it more—and was perched on the arm of a leather sofa, watching Poppy play Scrabble with the older maid and the chef. Josie was nowhere in sight, and neither were Rick or Mrs. Gallagher. I was sure the latter two were in the infirmary, but I had no idea where Josie might be. Blizz was also missing—she wasn't at Cody's side for once. I guessed she was probably in the infirmary keeping watch over Rick.

Stanley was already whining at Mr. Gallagher. I marched up to him.

"Don't believe a word he says," I said, glaring at Stanley. "You did all of it, didn't you?" I accused him. "The avalanche just now, the generator, the glass in the waffle . . ."

"You're crazy!" Stanley said again, sounding slightly hysterical. "I'm the victim here!"

"Right." Joe stepped forward. "The victim and the perpetrator. You're pretty much the only one who doesn't have an alibi for when the generator went out."

"What?" Mrs. Richmond spoke up. "But I thought the storm did that."

Mr. Gallagher looked grim. "Not exactly," he told the woman. "Boys, are you sure about this?"

"I believe we can prove he cut the generator lines yesterday," Joe said. "For one thing, Frank and I saw him leaving the kitchen a few minutes before it happened—probably about the time the chef's scissors went missing." He quickly explained about that incident.

Then I picked up the story. "Besides, it's simple process of elimination. When the power went out, most of us were right here." I glanced around, taking in the various guests and staff members.

"Not everybody," Stanley put in quickly. "I'm sure not everybody was here."

"What about the maids and Rick?" Nate spoke up. Everyone except the kids was gathered around us by now. "I don't think any of them were here. I remember, because I wanted to ask if they'd seen my book while they were working around the lodge."

"I can vouch for two of them," Poppy said, nodding at the older maid. "She was picking up the laundry from my room when it happened. And Rick was changing a lightbulb in my room."

"That's right," the maid said. "Miss Song and I had quite a lovely scream together when the lights went out. I'm not sure Rick was too amused." Both women smiled.

"What's going on out here?" Mrs. Gallagher said, appearing from the direction of the infirmary.

"How's Rick?" her husband asked.

"Cold. But he's okay."

That was a relief. Taking turns, Joe and Mr. Gallagher and I quickly filled her in.

"We're just figuring out if there was anyone except Stanley unaccounted for when the power went out," Mr. Gallagher added.

"What about Josie?" the chef said. "That girl's been missing in action most of the day. Including now."

"It wasn't Josie," Cody blurted out.

His father turned to look at him. "How do you know?" he asked.

Cody's face reddened. "I just know, okay? I—I was with her."

Mrs. Gallagher looked puzzled. "What?"

Before I knew it, Cody was confessing the whole Josie situation to his parents. They looked confused at first, and a bit disapproving about certain parts. But the actual Cody-and-Josie part? They looked kind of delighted about that.

"But this is wonderful," Mrs. Gallagher said. "You and Josie? How'd I miss that? And right under my nose, too!"

Her husband cleared his throat. "Er, we can discuss that later. Right now, let's focus on the situation at hand."

I noticed that Stanley was edging toward the door. Where did he think he was going? There was no escape out there. Not unless he had a snowmobile hidden outside.

Nate noticed him too. "Stop right there, pal," he said, stepping over and blocking Stanley's path. "Are you going to confess or what?"

"Who's going to make me?" Stanley sneered. Suddenly seeming to think better of the comment, he took a quick step back.

Everyone was staring at him. Mr. Gallagher looked very serious. "The phone lines are up and running again, and I expect the police will be able to get here before long," he said. "They'll have a few questions about all this."

He stepped forward and took Stanley by the arm. Nate grabbed the other arm.

"Hey!" Stanley protested, trying vainly to wiggle free. "Get your hands off me! I'll sue for assault!"

The two men dragged him away, ignoring his pleas and threats. Joe and I watched them go.

"Well," Joe said. "I suppose that's another case closed."

The local police arrived on snowmobiles within the hour. We weren't there for the interrogation, but Cody was. Afterward, he told us it hadn't been long before Stanley broke down and started confessing to most of the mischief.

"Stanley admitted to icing the steps, and putting the glass in the waffle batter," Cody said. He, Chet, Joe, and I were sipping hot cocoa in the otherwise deserted dining room. "He was planning to be the 'victim' of both those pranks himself so he'd have a concrete reason to sue the lodge. Apparently that's what he does—travels all across the country setting up 'accidents' and then suing for a boatload of money."

Joe made a face. "Classy."

"What about getting locked out in the storm?" I asked. "Was that a setup too?"

Cody nodded. "That too. Apparently that one almost went wrong in a big way. He was just going to lock himself out—he swiped a key from the office to do it—and then stay out long enough to look cold before he pounded on the door to come back in. And of course he had the key in case nobody heard him. But he misjudged how bad the storm was and ended up wandering out too far and getting disoriented." He dropped his hand to stroke Blizz, who was sitting quietly by his side. "So Blizz really did save his life that time."

"Wow." Joe whistled. "Stanley sabotaged the generator, too?"

Cody nodded. "That one was just to make the lodge look bad, I guess. He's the one who broke the kitchen window, too—apparently he slammed it down too hard after he tossed the scissors out. He also set up that avalanche on the ski shack roof, again planning to become the victim himself—only of course he knew when it was coming, so he could make sure it didn't totally bury him."

"That part was actually pretty slick," Chet said, his words still a little garbled. "I'm not sure I'd be able to rig up something like that."

"Yeah. Too bad Stanley uses his powers for evil instead of good." Joe looked puzzled. "There's one part I don't get, though. Why'd he hide Nate's book and the kid's boots and all that other stuff? Was that just making the lodge look bad again? Because it seems kind of petty compared to the rest."

"Dad asked him about that." Cody looked troubled. "Stanley insisted he didn't know anything about the missing stuff. Didn't even seem to realize it had turned up in that cabinet."

"Weird," I said. Then I shot Cody a sidelong look. Could he or Josie be the petty thieves? Maybe one of them had been trying to "un-frame" the other by snitching the stuff.

Either way, it didn't seem worth worrying about. Joe and I had solved the case.

By the time we finished breakfast the next morning, the road was officially open. Mr. Gallagher offered to drive Joe, Chet, and me to town when he went to officially press charges against Stanley down at the police station. After recovering from his ordeal, Rick had been so grateful to us for saving him that he'd offered to take a look at the jalopy. He'd quickly identified the part Chet needed and offered to help him fix it. We were planning to pick the part up in town, return to the lodge, and with any luck be on the road for Bayport Sweet Bayport right after lunch.

When we entered the lobby, Mr. Gallagher wasn't there yet, but Cody was straightening the magazines on a coffee table. Blizz was across the room, curled up in front of the fire.

"You guys getting ready to take off?" Cody asked.

"Yeah." Chet's voice sounded better, though he wasn't a happy camper about the liquid diet he was on until his cuts healed. "But we'll be back in a bit."

We were telling him about the jalopy situation when Poppy hurried into the lobby with her laptop tucked under her arm. She spotted Cody and stopped short, glancing around the room. Then she came forward more slowly.

"Listen," she said, her gaze skittering off toward the fire, then returning to Joe and me. "It's really amazing how you guys figured out what was going on around here. I'd love to interview you."

"Interview us?" I echoed. "What do you mean?"

"For my blog." Poppy held up the laptop. "I write for one of the big travel sites. That's why I'm here." She shrugged and smiled sheepishly. "I was supposed to be undercover, but I guess it won't hurt to reveal myself now."

"Undercover?" Suddenly things made a lot more sense. "So that's why you stayed when your friends left."

"Busted," she admitted cheerfully. "I thought about leaving too, but I wanted to see how the lodge handled the whole blizzard thing. Figured it would be a good angle for my article about the place."

"So that's why you were always asking so many questions," Joe said.

I nodded. Come to think of it, Poppy was pretty nosy. "Is that why you kept disappearing, too?" I asked, trying to figure out how that part fit in.

Poppy looked abashed. "Not exactly." Her gaze wandered toward the fireplace again. "I'm, um—sort of terrified of . . . dogs."

"Huh?" I glanced over at Cody's dog, who looked about as unthreatening as possible. "You mean like Blizz?"

"And Toy Toy." Poppy's face went red. "Size doesn't matter. They just freak me out. I'm not sure why."

As if sensing that we were talking about her, Blizz stood,

stretched, and wandered toward us. Poppy let out a squeak of fear.

"It's okay." Cody hurried over and took Blizz by the collar. "I've got her, see? She won't hurt you."

Poppy nodded, though she didn't look fully convinced. Keeping one eye on Blizz, she addressed Joe and me again. "So how about it?" she said. "Can I interview you? The Net would eat up the story of the teenage detectives who collared a criminal. You three would be famous!"

Chet smiled, seeming to like that thought. But Joe and I probably shouldn't let this story get out on the Internet, where everyone could see it.

"Um . . ." I thought fast. Glancing at Cody and Blizz, I smiled. "I have a better idea," I said, figuring I might as well kill two birds with one stone. "Why don't you do your article about Blizz?"

"The dog?" Poppy looked nervous. "What do you mean?"

Joe had caught on by now. "People love stories about animals," he told Poppy, echoing Cody's words to us the day before. "That could be your angle—hero dog saves the day! You could write about how she saved Stanley and also Rick."

I held my breath as Poppy studied Blizz—from a safe distance—with a little frown on her face. Would the dog-phobic journalist be convinced?

"I suppose you're right," she said after a moment, taking

a cautious half step forward. "Are you sure she's friendly?"

"Super friendly," Cody assured her. "Come closer—I'll keep hold of her if you want to try petting her."

Blizz's long pink tongue lolled out of her mouth as Poppy approached. If a dog could smile, that was what she was doing. Even Poppy seemed to sense it. She gave the dog a quick pat, then stepped back.

"Okay," she said with a nervous smile. "She does seem nice. . . ."

Spotting Mr. Gallagher coming in, we left Poppy shooting questions at Cody so fast he hardly had time to answer.

Mr. Gallagher saw us and jingled his keys. "Ready to go, boys?"

"We're ready," Chet said.

Just then Toy Toy trotted into the lobby, carrying a kid-size mitten. "Uh-oh," I said, shooting a look over at Poppy, who was typing away on her laptop as she and Cody talked. I didn't want the tiny dog to spook her just when she seemed ready to overcome her fear.

I stepped toward Toy Toy, planning to scoop him up and find Josie. But the tiny dog evaded me, dashing toward the cabinets by the fireplace.

"What's he doing?" Chet wondered.

My eyes widened as the poodle nosed open the lowest, narrowest cabinet door and deposited the mitten inside. Then he nudged the door shut again.

"It was Toy Toy!" I exclaimed with a laugh as the last puzzle piece snapped into place. "He's the petty thief! He must have started stealing stuff when Josie started letting him out around the guests more because of the blizzard."

Joe grinned. "Good work, bro," he said, raising his hand for a fist bump. "I guess that's another case closed!"